HEART
OF
SILVER
FLAME

Heart of Silver Flame

S D Simper

Heart of Silver Flame

Cover art by Jade Merien

Cover design and interior by Jerah Moss

Map by Mariah Simper

ISBN (Hardcover): 978-1-952349-15-7

Visit the author at www.sdsimper.com

Facebook: sdsimper
Twitter: @sdsimper
Instagram: sdsimper

For Andi

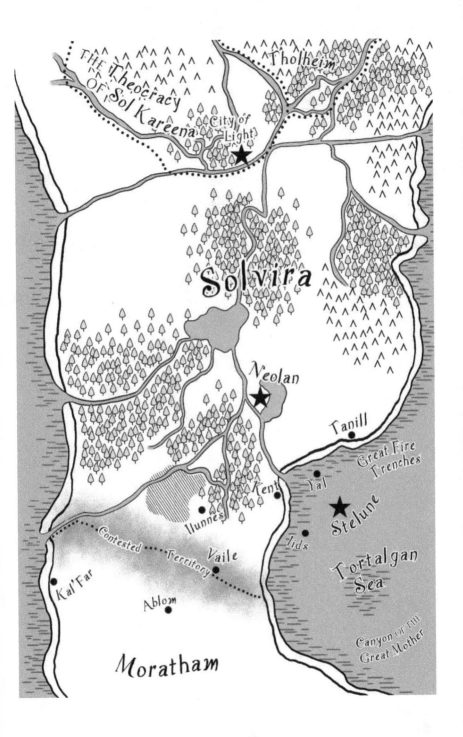

*One thousand years before the Old Gods return,
the Desert Sands conspires for a weapon . . .*

A weapon the Moon sealed away long ago.

Chapter I 🐚

The knife caught in the hinge of the oyster, and with a forceful twist the shell split in twain. Nestled in the meaty innards, Tallora plucked out a small pearl. She placed it in a basket, nearly filled to the brim with the valuable orbs, and moved on to the next, her endless task practiced and monotonous.

Beyond, she heard idle chatter—the voices of her mother and whatever customer had come into the front of the shop. Tallora, however, sat in the back room of her mother's store among a vast array of wares not yet prepared for display.

A slight ache coursed through her wrist as she twisted the knife, splitting the next oyster in the pile. The meat would be sold before the day was out, whereas the pearls would be cleaned and priced either individually or in bulk for the jewelers.

As she stabbed the next oyster at its hinge, a sudden uproar of yelling rose from outside the shop. Determined to ignore it, she clenched her jaw but missed the oyster's seam—narrowly missing her thumb next. Shock loosened her grip. The knife and oyster both gently floated to the table.

Though she could not quite decipher the words, her blood pulsed hot through her veins. Placing her wares aside, she peeked from the archway of the back room. She caught the eye of her mother, who chatted pleasantly with a customer, as though there weren't a small battalion of protestors across the canal outside.

The tension escalated every day.

Tallora swam through the beloved shop, past the wares stacked within alcoves, or tied down with nets lest they float away. They sold perishables, mostly—fish and edible seaweed, and occasionally foreign wares from the upper-world. As a small child, Tallora had been delighted by stories from above the

1

sea, thrilled to learn about the land and the food it provided—oddities such as apples and grapes and other strange plants. They spoiled quickly beneath the waves and thus sold for a high price.

But Tallora was no longer a child, and the mysteries of the world above the sea were no longer so mysterious. It had been six months since her return, yet she ached as though it was yesterday.

Closer now, she could hear the protestors' words. *"...Solvira has gone unpunished for atrocities for generations—how much longer until they seek to take the seas?"*

Tallora peeked outside the shop window and saw a gathered crowd watching a man screaming slander. *"They stole one of us; when will they steal all of us?"*

"Tallora—"

She turned, unsurprised to see her mother beside her. They bore the same features, mirrored in color from their pearlescent skin to the pinks of their tails, though instead of glimmering white, her mother's hair bore strands of grey, pulled back into a braided tail. Most hadn't been there...in the time before.

In the few months Tallora had been gone, her mother had aged at least six years.

"I know what you're thinking," her mother continued, gentleness in the subtle lines of her face. "You know it will do nothing."

"The monarch on their throne is the very monster who stole The Great Survivor! Will we live and die by her mercy alone?"

"No!"

Tallora gripped the doorframe, her fingers turning white. Her heartbeat pounded in her ears, deafening her to all but the hateful words.

"We cannot rest until Solvira's blood stains the sea! The Silver Fire shall reach its end!"

"Tallora—"

Tallora ignored the plea and swam from the shop.

Outside, buildings were stacked above and beside them, and before her lay an enormous canal, meant to direct the flow of swimming, lest the city fall into disarray. Carriages were pulled by large seahorses, some by dolphins—for the foolhardy—but most swam with merely their tails.

And across the flow of merfolk, there was a crowd of dissenters. *"The Solviraes seek to rule the land, but they shall never steal the seas!"*

The ensuing cheer only spurred her forward, and when she'd broken through the crowd, the man at the front—one she did not know—stared straight at her. "Friends, we have an unexpected visitor! Tallora, the Great Survivor herself—"

"Oh, shut *up* with that shit!" Tallora cried, and she swam beside the man to face the crowd. "I've told the story a thousand times, but still I hear it slandered in the streets! This fear-mongering will only push us into a war we can't possibly hope to win. Solvira has no intention of invading the seas! Solvira is hardly innocent, but they've made amends for their crimes, and Goddess Staella herself forgave Empress Dauriel Solviraes—I was there!" Tallora gazed upon the stunned onlookers, her jaw trembling, heart racing. "The empress will not harm the Tortalgan Sea, and I will stake my honor on that statement. She has no quarrel with us! And I have no quarrel with her. I forgave her—" Her voice cracked; by Staella's Grace, she *would not cry.* "There is no crime."

She saw their faces. She knew their thoughts. The rumors were like scattered sand across the beach—

"I heard she was raped by the empress and forced into chains . . ."

"Morathma himself decreed she be set free . . ."

"She was enchanted by their sorcery—her mind is no longer her own."

. . . to try and collect them was foolhardy.

"You needn't lie to save face," the leader said, loud enough for all to hear. "Solvira cannot hear you—"

"Oh, fuck off." Tallora swam away. Not to her shop, lest they follow. But straight up, toward the light, toward the sun warming the waves.

Her mother had spoken true. It would do nothing. She'd returned to the sea as the very picture of innocence, stolen and ruined by a tyrannical shadow, and no matter how much she pled and screamed, it was all they saw her as.

The 'Great Survivor' she might be, but they did not see her as a survivor. Only a victim.

Tallora broke from the waves, the cool air brisk and invigorating. She brushed the hair from her face, her long locks clinging to her skin. The sun shone bright, and the open sea stretched in every direction— no land, no boats. Nothing to disrupt the perfect horizon.

Tallora loved her home. She loved the open waves. She brought up her tail and floated on the surface, her scales and chest warmed by the light. It might have been bliss, but angry tears welled in her eyes, nonetheless. She let them flow free. There was no one to judge. Tallora was truly alone—

A hand touched her back. "Tallora—"

She shrieked, doubling over to defend her stomach, but she knew that mop of navy hair and those laughing eyes. "Fuck you, Kal."

The man smiled, and Tallora's anger seeped away. After Tallora had bowed before King Merl and relayed her tale and offered Solvira's apology, his eldest son, Prince Kalvin, had made it his mission to befriend her . . . and succeeded.

"You made quite the scene down there," Kal said, but his face held no judgement. Instead, he spread his arms wide, conveying an innocent offering. "Are you all right?"

Tallora nodded and accepted the hug, finding peace in his presence and certainly not ignorant to the

4

strength in his biceps. She let it help rewrite the memory of a different embrace, strong and lithe from years of wielding double blades. "You know I hate that shit. I know I should let it go, but . . ."

How dare they slander the woman I love.

"I can't stand their lies," she finished instead.

She had told the truth to anyone who would listen, saving only one beloved and damning piece for herself—that she had loved and had been loved by the woman they hated, the very image of Solvira's bloodlust. The Solviraes bloodline held insanity in its incestuous lineage, evident in their brutal, tyrannical legacies, yet some of their rulers held wisdom unparalleled, their godly progenitors made manifest. The world watched Dauriel Solviraes, slandered her name, yet there was fear beneath the rage.

Kal didn't release her until she pulled away. "There're always protestors over something," he said unhelpfully, but his earnest expression suggested he meant well. "They'll forget and find something else to hate. When we were children, it was the Onians. Now, it's Solvira. In a few years, it'll be Zauleen—or who knows."

"I know," Tallora said, gazing up at the sky. Evening would fall in a few hours. Then, the stars would glitter across the sky.

"What's the worst that can happen?"

"I don't know. Likely nothing."

Kal offered his arm, his smile kind. "May I escort you back?"

Tallora shook her head. "My mother will be furious, but I can't go to the shop. Everything is . . ."

She shut her eyes, and there again were their jeers, their hateful words, and worst of all, their pity. She, the victim, the conquest of Solvira. Once upon a time, she'd been told words that still pushed her to tears at night: *"I would have made you my empress."*

". . . much too loud," she said simply. "I think I need to be alone."

"Without me?"

He pouted like a sad puffer fish, and Tallora's smile came unbidden. "You don't count as company."

Kal placed a hand on his heart in mock offense. "Woe is me. I am no one and shall die as no one."

When she laughed, so did he. "You're something, that's for certain," she said between giggles. She stole his hand from his chest, imagining calluses where his were soft from the salt and water. "Take me somewhere fun, then. But away from Stelune."

He led her to a coral reef filled with life and color and all the beauty of the sea. He laughed at the clownfish, tickled her with kelp, and for a moment, Tallora forgot the knot in her stomach, content to merely bask in the sights and sounds.

Kal was perfect. He was the most beautiful man she'd ever seen, endlessly endearing as he cupped a little fish in his hands and gently spoke of how lovely it was. Oh, she so desperately wanted to want him. The fish swam away, and she was left with his smile and the delightful sparkle in eyes.

They laughed until nightfall, and then he swam her home, the streets having largely cleared of merfolk. Instead, globes of light were suspended above the stone lamps, manufactured by the sorcerers who worked for the palace. "Tomorrow is the blood moon," Kal said, diverting the subject away from their jests. "My cousin will be hosting a party at the Great Fire Trenches. Apparently, the entire trench turns red beneath its light. You'll come with me, won't you?"

He still held her hand. It felt pleasant, but not sensational. She intertwined their fingers, hoping to ignite a spark. Nothing. "Sounds like a scandal. I thought only Onians danced beneath the blood moon."

"I thought you liked being in the center of a scandal."

The statement might have offended her, but Kal never said anything maliciously. "You have me

6

there," she replied with a wink. "I'll go. You'll have to escort me, though."

They stopped before her door, the home she shared with her mother. "I'll be here at sunset." Kal's smile lit up the night, and when he lingered, Tallora's chest tightened.

She offered a quick hug. "Goodnight!"

And before he could reply, she rolled aside the thin stone set before the home, slipped inside, and pulled it shut. Against the door, she released her held breath.

The modest home bore only three rooms. She swam down to the one set aside for her. Her bedroom held a stone slab for sleeping, now with a woven disc of kelp to cushion her head—pillows were an uplander tradition she had come to love. Every bit of wall-space was covered in jewelry or shells, or some pretty thing she'd found as a youth. A mirror on the wall stood taller than she—hanging from it was a forgotten vestment of Staella, her quest to become a priestess abandoned. The pearls and sea stars, strung into a lengthy necklace, had once been her dearest possession. To look upon it stung, the weight too much for her to carry.

A small table held accessories for her hair and tailfin. Tucked away beside the mirror was a small, rectangular box. Tallora opened its lid, revealing a pair of simple shears.

She knew what Kal wanted. He had told her as much before, confessed that he found her beautiful and wanted to know her better. And she had told him the truth: *"I'm not ready, I'm sorry. I need to learn how to be myself again before I can even consider—"*

And by every god in Celestière—she wanted to move on. She lifted the shears into her hands, but instead of Kal's blue mop, she saw a braid of onyx fall to the floor.

By Staella's Grace, she wanted to want to love him. She wanted to gaze into his eyes and return the affection she saw there, kiss his beautiful lips and feel a spark, let him fill the void in her soul.

It was her heart that dragged its tail along the ocean floor, remiss to be anything but a burden. Tallora held the shears and wept.

In the morning, the sun cast filtered daylight through the waves, but Tallora's mind felt dark.

"Tallora, you're my daughter," her mother said in the shop, "but you're also a grown woman and my employee. You can't go swimming away in the middle of the day!" Between customers exiting and entering, Tallora's mother fell into a testy rant. "Where did you even go? You disappeared after you made your scene across the way."

"I was out." Tallora straighten the arrangement of salmon on the slab—a delicacy, given the fish swam in fresh water. Though hesitant to admit the truth, she finally said, "Out with Kal. He took me to Elanva's Reef to cheer me up."

She was met with silence. When she finally turned from the display of fish, her mother had busied herself with counting coins at the front. Yet, the forced grit of her jaw revealed the tension beneath. Tallora set aside her wares and cautiously approached. "Momma—"

"You worry me." Red rimmed her mother's eyes, but when Tallora tried to speak, she waved away her words. "I'm sorry. I shouldn't let anxiety get the better of me. Whenever you disappear, I just know they've taken you again." Her voice broke at the last word; she turned instead to the alcoves of wares.

Tallora forgot the salmon and joined her mother instead, placing a gentle hand on her bare waist. "No, I'm sorry. You're right." When her mother pulled her into a tight hug, Tallora clung to her. "I'm right here."

They lapsed into silence, and when her mother pulled away, she cupped Tallora's cheek. "It hurts me to see you hurting."

"I'm not—"

"Tallora," she gently chided, and her smile held the weight of all the months Tallora had been missing. "Tallora, my little guppy, you put on a brave face. But yesterday told me this is still eating at you."

Today, she had awoken with a weight on her chest, and she knew not if it was the nightmare of the ambassador's hands on her body or the memory of Dauriel's embrace protecting her. The touch grew fainter every night. "I'm trying to move past it."

"I've told you time and time again—the temple is filled with priestesses trained to help ease emotional burdens."

Tallora shook her head. "It's not what I need." Perhaps it was, but if she couldn't say the whole truth, what use was there?

"When is the last time you prayed?" her mother asked. "Sincerely prayed? Staella is a Goddess of Comfort."

A few scattered times, though she didn't say those words aloud. Never at the temple—it bore the reminders of her discarded dreams of joining the priestesses there. But beneath the starry sky, she had prayed a few times at the surface, finally grasping at peace . . . until, one night, a ship had sailed across the horizon, bombarding Tallora with memories both cherished and feared.

Beneath the waves, she'd disappeared, and since then had kept her silence. Here in her mother's shop, she merely shrugged, hoping the matter could be set aside.

Her mother released her, reticence in her pose. "I'm here, if you ever want to talk."

She did. She so desperately did, though she wondered if her mother could accept the truth—that her daughter loved the empress of a hated nation.

"Mom . . ." Her tongue faltered—not for shame but for fear. Perhaps a muted version of the truth instead. "There is something—something I've told no one about." Her mother's searching eyes saw nothing, for the truth was too outlandish to guess. Pressure swelled in Tallora's chest, longing for release. "There was a spot of joy in Solvira, someone I had to leave behind and never see again. Her name . . ."

"Oh, Dauriel, my empress . . ."

". . . her name was Leah. She was one of the courtesans, and I have never loved anyone like I loved her."

The lie didn't matter; the words ruptured the tight ball in her chest. Tallora's hands covered her face when the first of her sobs wracked her body.

Her mother left for only a moment, to shut the door of the shop. When she returned to Tallora's side, she held her in a tight embrace. "I didn't want anyone to think," Tallora managed between sobs, "that I had been manipulated into speaking well of Solvira, so we resolved to tell no one about it once I left. I have to forget her, but my heart still feels like it's a thousand miles away."

Mother's hand stroked soothing lines into her white locks. "I'm sorry you've had to go through this alone." Tallora felt a kiss in her hair. "Won't you tell me about her? I want to know everything."

They settled in by the wall. "She was cruel at first," Tallora said, the admittance welling fresh hurt in her lungs, staunching her easy breaths, "yet we came to be friends. We never should have fallen in love, but she's the one who saved me from the Morathan Ambassador when he was supposed to sleep with me. She risked everything to protect me from Empress Vahla. Her love was sincere. She proved it in all she did."

10

She spoke of light and love, of their cruel beginning and heartbreaking end—all that she could without revealing Dauriel's true identity. By the end, she lay with her head in her mother's lap, idly watching her tailfin float in the still water. Mother's fingers wove tender lines through her hair. "I've done all I can to move on," Tallora finished, "but I'm still hurting."

"Is that why you've attached yourself to Kal?"

"More like he's attached himself to me, but . . ." She shut her eyes, remembering Kal's hand in hers. "Yes. I like Kal. I love spending time with him, and I think I could love him. I *want* to fall for him."

"It would be a charmed life, to be his queen."

But not his empress. Tallora idly stroked her finger along her mother's scales, finding comfort in the pattern.

"But you can't force yourself to fall in love, and you haven't a hope when you still love that girl in Solvira."

"Then what do I do?" Tallora looked up into her mother's wise eyes and saw her sad smile reflected downward.

"You need more time. And that's awful to say, because I know you want it to be over and done with, but if you truly love this girl, you have to hurt to heal. And you will. Time heals everything. But the time isn't over yet."

Tallora nodded, her heart aching, but her soul felt lighter by subtle degrees. "How long did it take you to heal?"

Behind her mother's smile were threatened tears. Tallora's papa was a weight wherever they went—not a burden, no. But a presence. "I'll let you know, once the healing is done."

When silence settled, they broke apart. They reopened the shop. Tallora returned to her duties, her lungs finally able to draw breath.

Chapter II 🐚

The Great Fire Trenches held the entrance to a cave myth said led to the core of the realm. Others said it was a monster's tomb and the winding maze of caves were carved, meant to detour the foolhardy from finding it. A river of molten rock ran through the bottom, sending blasts of hot water through cracks in the walls and bubbles of searing heat into the boiling hot springs. The dangerous terrain held beauty, yes, but had also claimed countless lives over the centuries—from reckless drunkards daring to touch the molten floor to small children wandering into the caves and never returning.

Naturally, it became a popular attraction.

That evening, Tallora followed Kal, laughing all the while. The Trench was an hour's swim from Stelune, and despite the uplifting mood, anxiety rang like a bell in her head. For six months, she'd been a shut-in; a small piece of her hoped this would be the beginning of something better.

"You said your cousin is hosting this party?" she asked when the trench came into view. Riotous revelers laughed at the bottom, some dancing, others enjoying the hot springs.

"Correct. Duke Raileigh of Black Reef. But don't call him that. Just call him 'Duke.'"

Tallora chuckled, unimpressed at this apparently eccentric gentleman. "Really?"

"He's a bit of a loon, but my uncle lets him throw all the money he wants into parties, so he's a good man to keep around." Kal swam ahead; Tallora raced to follow.

The heat rose the deeper they swam, but for all the hazards of this place, no one had actually boiled to death. Yet. The brilliant hints of red peeking beneath the expanding cavern served as an ominous warning. The sight was unquestionably beautiful, the craggy terrain too hot for life. No plants could grow here, so there remained only cliffs of stark black rock.

To combat the ominous aura, Tallora focused instead on the partiers and the trays of gelatinous bait—colorful, sweetened, and fermented. She'd tried wine once during her days above land and found it bitter. Bait served the same purpose, to intoxicate your senses and loosen your tongue, but held sweetness to combat its bite.

She recognized quite a few in the crowd, each of them somewhere in the nebulous realm between 'acquaintance' and 'friend.' In the time before, during Tallora's carefree days, she might've called them the latter—her mother had once teased that she'd partied with half the ocean. But in her six months of isolation, not a single person had reached out.

All she'd had was Kal.

"Duke!" Kal suddenly cried, and a well-built merman swam to greet him, the family resemblance apparent in their similarly-hued hair and skin—blue and tanned. They embraced a moment, then Kal gestured to her. "This is my friend, Tallora."

Duke lacked the sharp eyes and quick smile of his cousin—instead he stared with a hint of dopiness. Perhaps that was merely the bait. "Tallora? The Great Survivor?"

It took all her willpower to bite back a groan at the title. She cracked a smile, praying it didn't look too forced. "Well, I am Tallora, and I certainly survived something, but I wouldn't say I did a great job of it—"

"Betr! Rand!" Duke beckoned to a nearby group—both men and the ladies accompanying them joined their party. "This is Tallora, the Great Survivor."

"Well, fuck me," she said pleasantly, but her smile curtailed her ire. Hopefully. "Yes, that's me. I went to Solvira, and now I'm here."

13

Despite her palpable discomfort, they peppered her with questions—though she did try to answer: "Is Solvira as big as they say?"

"Likely bigger," she replied. "It expands the land from the Tortalgan Sea to the Onian."

"Is it true the royals fuck their siblings?"

Tallora grimaced at that but nodded. "Empress Vahla was married to her cousin, but apparently that's happened too."

"I've heard there are life-size statues to Staella."

"Likely true, though I can't personally confirm it."

"But did you really see the Goddess of Stars?"

Tallora simply nodded and politely refused to speak more of it. "It's personal, but I can confirm that it happened."

"Is it true the princess has the face of an angler fish?"

Glass shattered in Tallora's mind. The forced niceties of her disposition faded. "I beg your pardon?"

The unfortunate object of her scrutiny was Duke himself. "Rumor says she's not exactly a gem in the Solviran Crown, if you know what I mean." He turned to his friend—Rand, she would have guessed, but she couldn't remember in that moment. Not when confronted with slander. "I heard she once raped a girl at a party and tried to kill herself after."

"What?!" she cried, her pleasantness rapidly evaporating. "That's a shit claim, so don't fucking spread it! Empress Dauriel would never, so kindly fuck off!"

Unfortunately, despite the teasing appall among their small crowd, Duke didn't look offended. Worse, he said, "Damn, Kal—you always pick the feisty ones."

They laughed, though Kal's was notably nervous, and Tallora forced a smile and excused herself, feigning the need for bait.

Well, she did plan on taking bait but more wanted to distance herself from the poisoned words.

How dare they? How *dare* they speak so cruelly of the most painful moment in Dauriel's life!? She plucked a gelatinous ball from a woman holding a platter, swallowing it whole before she felt a hand on her waist. Kal appeared at her side. "Are you all right?"

"Old wounds," she said simply. "I don't want to talk about it."

"Tallora!"

Tallora turned at the familiar voice. "Juliae?"

Tallora might've once said that Juliae was the loveliest girl she'd ever met, with dark hair the color of undersea trenches and a subtle purple hue to her skin. They weren't quite friends, but they had once swapped a few drunk kisses at a similar event a year or so back. When they embraced, Tallora noticed her entourage—other girls she swore she'd partied with before. Juliae smiled and said, "Look at you, leaving the house!"

Tallora laughed at the tease. "You have me there."

"Does this mean we'll get to hear your drunk rendition of *Tortalga the Great* again?"

Tallora blushed, because apparently six months and a few more in Solvira hadn't rid the world of that memory. "With enough bait, anything is possible."

Juliae laughed, as did Kal, though there was no way he knew what they were talking about. "Prince Kalvin, I didn't know you were with her."

Tallora frowned at the implication, but Kal said, "We met in my father's court, as unappealing as that sounds. But I knew I had to get to know her, as soon as I saw her."

"We're very good friends," Tallora quickly added, content to kill that rumor before it had a chance to come to life.

Juliae and Tallora shared *the look*—the look only women could share when they were having a secret conversation about a man they didn't want the man understanding—and it seemed Juliae understood precisely what Tallora meant. "Well, take your bait and come dance with us! My intended is coming later with a bunch of his friends—I think you'd like them."

They said a quick farewell, but truthfully Tallora did not want to meet anyone's friends. Still, it was considerate of her to offer to introduce her to men other than Kal.

"You're a popular woman," Kal said, amusement lighting his features.

Tallora shrugged. "Popularity doesn't mean friendship—"

"Tallora!"

Tallora didn't know the small group of girls who came to greet her, but she laughed along with them all the same, realizing her reputation had apparently preceded her. They giggled around Kal, shameless in their flirtation, yet he remained friendly and unobtainable; Tallora knew full well what he wanted.

But as the girls fawned over his jests, Tallora caught sight of two woman in their own little world, nestled in one of the hot springs—one with cropped hair who kissed her partner with all the tenderness in the world.

Her heart ached.

When Kal offered her another piece of bait, she accepted, hoping the ease of drunkenness would subdue her soon.

With time it did, and as she floated among gaggles of partygoers, danced in a crowd much too close to the burning crevices, her senses steadily dulled. Solvira and all its pain slowly slipped away, replaced with sensation and lights and her own blurring sight.

She danced with Juliae, flirted with her entourage, swapped jests she wouldn't remember when her mind cleared. When Juliae flittered away, distracted by the arrival of her man, Tallora pulled Kal in to dance, adoring his smiling, full lips, uncaring of the bait on his breath. They danced long enough for her vision to steady, though the aftereffects of drunkenness lingered in her dizzy head. When he stole her hand, she interlaced their fingers, pretending they were long and lithe, and when he pulled her to one of the hot springs, she settled in with a laugh, finding his words charming, his jests hilarious. In the warmth of the bubbling trench, his embrace was warmer still, and she might've contentedly settled in his arms for hours, but then his lips brushed hers.

For a moment, she succumbed. Amidst the lights and joyous revelry, she could forget who she was and savor the feeling of lips on her own, of hands on her waist and in her hair. She dared to peek, and in the moments before her vision steadied, those dark locks held an auburn tint, subtle femininity in those cheekbones.

She blinked and there was Kal, beautiful, perfect Kal, a prince and a man utterly smitten by her. Gently, she pushed him away. "We talked about this," she whispered, and she couldn't face his dejection.

"I'm sorry," she heard. "I thought I read the mood properly."

"You did." Feeling foolish, feeling vain, she floated up, surprised when his large hand stole hers. "Kal—"

"You're not ready. I know." He floated up so their faces were level, kindness in his gaze. "But I want to be here when you are. You're worth the wait."

A sincere smile twisted her lips. "You're a good man, Kal."

"You're healing. I respect that. If you ever need to talk . . ." He gestured to himself, his shrug too darling for words. "I'm here for you."

When he pulled her in for a hug, she accepted the gesture, finding peace in his embrace. "Thank you." She forced a smile. "Perhaps someday."

She hoped the words didn't sting. Judging by Kal's endearing smile and gesture to return to the party, she supposed they hadn't.

As they swam away from their private pool, a sudden vibration rippled through the water.

The cavern rumbled. The walls shook. Bits of debris loosened from the cliffs. Speckled bits of black dust misted the waters, polluting the cavern.

A hush filled the party-goers. From somewhere far below, Tallora heard the rumbling of thunder beneath the earth.

The cavern shook, enormous jutting stones suddenly thrusting from the walls. Screams filled the canyon—some merfolk were trapped, others battered by falling rocks. Tallora could hardly see through the dusty debris, so when a familiar hand clutched her wrist to drag her away, she trusted it.

Another violent shock jolted through the canyon. Kal wrenched her away from the walls— just as a boulder might've crushed her.

In a moment too tense for words, Tallora grabbed his arm and swam downward. The cave swallowed them whole just as falling rocks blockaded their exit.

Darkness engulfed them.

Tallora coughed as she was plunged into darkness. Dirt expelled from her lungs, the water absolutely saturated in it, thick and vile whenever she breathed. Hot, stagnant water coiled around her, confining in the pitch-black space.

"Are you all right?" came Kal's voice, his hand tightly squeezing hers.

"Yes," Tallora managed to say in the midst of her coughing fit. "What in Onias' Hell was that?"

Kal squeezed her hand, his presence a comfort to her racing heart. "I don't know. But we have to find a way out of here."

Tallora nodded, then realized he couldn't see the gesture. "Move slowly. Hands on the wall."

Kal took the lead, releasing her hand and instead pulling her close to his side. She presumed he kept a touch on the wall as he swam, but utter darkness clouded her view. On instinct, Tallora held a hand in front, lest they swim into a wall. In the oppressive darkness, her panicked heart raced, expecting any moment to be eaten by a shark or crushed by a collapsing wall. Beyond, she heard the ominous rumble of stone and earth, muted in their underground prison.

Light began as a pinprick. Kal picked up speed, releasing Tallora as they darted toward it.

The narrow cave suddenly opened up into a great pit, and far below Tallora saw evidence of molten lava. The heat rose, even hundreds of feet above.

From below rang a great *shriek*.

Tallora covered her ears, darting to the center of the enormous cavern when the walls shook. The top held no exit; only darkness. Instead, as the cacophonous noise settled down, she grabbed Kal's hand and dragged him down, toward the burning depths.

The cavern, she realized, was a tunnel—the base of it, hundreds of feet above the pit of lava, expanded into a far larger cave, capable of housing a small city.

A subtle glow of red shone from the molten pit in the center. The lava bubbled and churned, as though recently unsettled, and Tallora wondered how they were not boiling alive. But greater light shone from illuminate spheres, held at the end of staves—they were not alone in this cave.

Tallora pressed herself against the topmost base of the tunnel and held a finger to her lips at Kal before she peered down.

Far below, she saw a struggling figure upon the shore, tied with ropes—perhaps the source of the screaming. Great rocks lay scattered beside her, the dust freshly disturbed. The figure bore a tentacled lower half, ten sleek appendages undulating in the water, a few attempting to free her of her bonds. She was unquestionably an Onian. Merfolk were descendants of Tortalga; Onians claimed the demon god Onias as their progenitor. The woman held a larger physique, more suited to northern climates, but her skin gave Tallora pause—it perfectly matched the black earth, yet reflected the red glow of the lava as she moved.

Tallora came to her senses and darted down, Kal in tow. Horrid lacerations covered the Onian woman's body, too deliberate to be accidental.

Tallora stopped, however, at the massive mural before them.

Carved into the stone, larger than she herself, was a single, gigantic eye, surrounded by a swirling mass of what might have been tentacles. The spacious wall stood hundreds of feet high, spanning even wider, with runes written upon the sides, though she could not read them.

Still, that eye followed wherever she went, the sight filling her with dread. There was something familiar about it, yet her mind couldn't fathom where she had seen the image before.

She gasped when a hand grabbed her wrist. Kal swam in front of her. "Sorry—"

"You're fine," she said, returning her attention to the woman below. She darted downward, her bleeding heart longing to help. "Are you all right?"

The Onian's single eye suddenly stared. It dominated her face, larger than even her wide, inhuman mouth, and glowed in blood-red hues. "Who are you?"

Her words held a deep, guttural tone—unquestionably demonic, reminding Tallora of Solvira's general. "My name is Tallora. There was an earthquake, and we ended up in this cave."

Though the Onian lay on the shore, her arms and tentacles tied with ropes, she still managed to look imposing as she glared. "Call me Harbinger. Who is the boy?"

"I am Prince Kalvin, Son of Merl," Kal said, concern in his tone. "Will you let us help you?"

Harbinger offered her tied arms in response. Tallora joined Kal in attempting to release her, the loosened ropes revealing more brutal slashes across her body. Slow and bitter work, but soon enough Tallora pulled the first of the ropes away. "What happened to you?" she asked.

Harbinger stared at the ceiling, the sneer at her lips revealing rows of pointed teeth. Somehow, her silver hair never seemed to float into her eye. "I came into the company of bad men. They thought I knew things. I do know things, but not the things they wanted."

"But why?" Tallora said, her heart aching at the gruesome display. "Oh by Staella's Grace, please tell us if we hurt you."

"All of me hurts. Little more you can do." Harbinger's scowl darkened the room—perhaps literally, if the flickering shadows weren't a trick of the light. "I told you why. They thought I knew things."

"Where are they now?" Tallora pressed, finally liberating Harbinger's arms of the ropes. She joined Kal in trying to free her tentacles.

Harbinger stretched her arms, though it only revealed the extent of the damage, the brutal lacerations, as well as what appeared to be a raw brand on one forearm. "They are still here. Not so much a danger anymore." She looked toward one of the massive, fallen rocks, and Tallora's gut clenched when she saw a hint of a bloodied tailfin peeking from beneath.

21

"T-The earthquake," she said, blood running cold at the ghastly sight. "That was you."

"Correct. I apologize for any inconvenience. Did not know there would be merfolk here."

There had been many merfolk in the area, but Tallora swallowed that for now, unwilling to risk tears. She knew not if they were dead or if they'd escaped the calamity. "Kal and I are fine, though we aren't certain if we can escape."

"Oh, easy," Harbinger replied, and when the last of her tentacles was finally freed, she stretched them out, slowly floating upward. Her skin changed to match, shifting to become the same deep blue of the water. "I will escort you out, as my thanks. I find little kindness among you merfolk, so I am surprised but grateful."

Kal swam toward the glimpse of gory remains. "Who were they?"

Harbinger joined him; if she were affected by her injuries, she hid it well. "I would love to tell you, Prince of the Tortalgan Sea, but I am cursed to secrecy." She held out her arm, revealing the gnarled brand on her wrist. It bore a runic design, reeking of magic, its presence oddly sickening. "I can say nothing of it. A pity, because there are some I did not kill," she continued, bitterness on her tongue. "Those were the ones present today."

Kal glanced warily between Harbinger's burn and her eerie countenance. "Are my people in danger?"

Harbinger stared thoughtfully a moment, her single eye imposing. "Not assuredly."

"Is there anything you can tell us?"

Again, Harbinger fell into silence, her mouth occasionally twitching from unspoken words. "I will think on that," she said cryptically, and Tallora fought to hide her frown—this woman had clearly been wronged, but her words hid behind layers of secrecy. "Follow me. I will escort you out."

"Before you do," Tallora interrupted, swimming toward the mural, "what is this place?"

"A den of great evil," Harbinger replied, visage darkening. Tallora swore her eye flashed. "I cannot say much more."

Tallora nodded, then followed when the Onian beckoned.

At the cusp of darkness, Harbinger held out a hand. She released a breath, and an orb of pure light floated in her palm. "Stay close."

Eerie light flickered across the cave wall as they swam, the shadows constantly shifting in Harbinger's presence. Still, Tallora was grateful to not have to navigate dark waters. "You must be a witch," she said, though she saw no evidence of a familiar.

"Yes and no. I was born with strong magic. My pledge to Onias simply gave me more."

Those pledged to demons were granted power in the form of an animal companion—as were those pledged to angels, but the stigma was ... different. "Where's your familiar?"

"Hopefully at home, and not stupidly trying to track me down. Drak'Thon hid when I was captured, and thank Onias' Glory. I would be ruined without him." Her eye squinted, the camouflaging hues of her skin eerie as she took on the color of the light. "Prince Kalvin of the Tortalgan Sea ..." Harbinger muttered softly, but before the prince in question could respond, she stopped and turned her enormous eye to Tallora, her stare a thousand miles away. "Tallora ..." Her gaze narrowed, a subtle smile twisting her lip. "Daughter of Myalla. You are the girl they whisper about, the one stolen by Solvira."

"That's correct," she said, praying her grimace was properly subdued.

"Interesting," Harbinger mused, but she continued on her way.

Unnerved at the interaction, Tallora looked to Kal for a reaction, but her friend had fallen into contemplative silence.

The winding cave seemed aimless, and several times they reached a split in the path—only for Harbinger to forge onward with no hesitation. Tallora found this strange, but she found many things about this new companion strange and resolved to ask a few pointed questions once they came to safety.

Witches were feared, their demonic patrons highly distrusted, and Tallora wondered how much Harbinger truly knew . . . and what she kept to herself by choice instead of by force.

Tallora couldn't begin to guess how much time they'd spent in the dark tunnels, but when blessed light shone far ahead, it took all her self-control to not bolt toward it.

The cavern ended at the cusp of open waters. She nearly sobbed for joy, leaving Kal and Harbinger and twirling about in the boundless sea.

But she just as quickly stopped. By Staella's Grace—she had no idea where they'd ended up. The dark ocean spread before them, empty as far as the eye could see. Behind she saw a great mountain range—the cave from whence they'd come. Thankfully, the black sky bespoke the presence of stars; perhaps the constellations would bring them home.

The light in Harbinger's hand extinguished; her skin became the color of the sea. When she smiled, her pointed teeth reminded Tallora of the predatory sharks of the depths. "Safe and sound."

When Kal flashed his charming, princely smile and offered a hand, Harbinger stared at it a full three seconds before hesitantly grabbing it with her own. "You have the thanks of the crown of the Tortalgan Sea," Kal said. "My father will surely reward you for saving our lives."

"You saved mine first, so Demoni Law says all is equal." She took back her hand, her refractive eye difficult to read. But she kept her smile and said, "But *tell* your king. And . . . if you are so grateful, perhaps you would allow me a final boon?"

Kal nodded. "Anything within my power, I will give."

She held his stare as she smiled. In a single, fluid motion, she reached up and grabbed a small tuft of his hair and *yanked.*

Kal flinched and rubbed the afflicted spot. "I beg your pardon?"

"This is my boon," Harbinger said, and between her fingers were a few strands of unmistakable navy blue hair. "I like you, Prince Kalvin. You send your father my regards." She looked to Tallora. "May I?"

Tallora protectively gathered the flowing locks of pure white hair. "Why?"

"You are a chosen of Staella, yes?"

"Am I .. ?"

"She is at least liking you. There is power that comes from being favored of a goddess." Harbinger held out a hand, and Tallora felt a stirring in her gut, clenching and screaming *no.*

Witches were feared for a reason. "With all possible respect, I'd rather not," she said, forcing as sincere a smile as she could muster.

Harbinger frowned, and the pointed teeth made it far more frightening than she perhaps intended. Still, the sight sent chills along Tallora's arms. "All right. Your choice."

She looked back to Kal, visibly intrigued as she said, "If you run into trouble, you can find me in Eel Reef. That path shall be opened to you—but do not be alarmed when it appears. You are welcome there." She spared a glance upward, toward the surface high above. "Followers of Staella know the stars, yes? You can find your way home?"

"Yes, but . . ." Tallora fought to hide her frown, but all her nerves were alight. ". . . how do you know I'm a follower of Staella?"

"I meet new people, and Onias whispers." Mischief twisted her lip, though it appeared as more of a sneer than a smile. "Before I go to lick my wounds, I have contemplated this so listen well. My captors . . ." Her lips suddenly pursed, as though forced shut by an outside force. She muttered unintelligibly for a few seconds, then finally her words burst free once more. "They seek the key to a weapon—a weapon more powerful and dangerous than any other. I thought I knew nothing of it; now I am not so certain." She looked to Tallora, any lingering amusement fading from her countenance. "You reek of Silver Flame. You be careful." Then to Kal, she said, "You tell your father. Tell him *I* saved you." She swam back, just out of arm's reach. "Farewell."

Though unnerved at Harbinger's words, Tallora returned the sentiment, waiting until the Onian vanished before looking to Kal. "She's clearly been wronged, but there's more to this. She knew too much about us."

"Onias is a God of Knowledge and Secrets," Kal said, his gaze lingering where Harbinger had left. "Why wouldn't he talk to her?"

Oh, Kal. Always thinking the best of people. Tallora finally released her hair, unwilling to say more of her reservations about the witch's character. Instead, she glanced around the open water and then to the surface, just able to see the moon's light, distorted and bright. "Follow me."

As a follower of Staella, Goddess of Stars, Tallora had learned long ago the names of stars and constellations, their positions in the sky, the stories they told, and how to follow their lead.

So when she burst forth from the depths, the wind and night air invigorating upon her skin, the celestial lights above promised a way home. "We'll have to stay near the surface," she said, "but we're only a few hours from Stelune."

Chapter III 🐚

They travelled in silence for a time, until Tallora remembered something that would surely haunt her. "That mural on the wall," she muttered, her skin cold at the thought, "what did you think of it?"

"It was terrifying," Kal replied. They were mere inches beneath the water, the wind abrasive on their tails, but easily able to glance up and check their location. "I don't read Demoni though, so I can't say much more."

Tallora whispered, "I've seen it before. I *know* I have, but I don't know when. Or how. Much less what it means. But, Kal, we've stumbled across something we weren't supposed to see, and I fear there's something evil stirring."

"I'll speak to my father," Kal said, the earnest resolve in his voice nothing less than charming. "If there are wicked men capturing innocent witches, he needs to know."

"I don't know that she's innocent," Tallora said, remiss to forget the earthquake. "She knows more than she's saying, even beyond her curse."

"I'm far more concerned about this 'weapon' Harbinger mentioned," Kal replied, his thoughtful expression furrowing his handsome brow. "What weapon could possibly be hidden beneath the ocean?"

Tallora briefly lifted her head above the water to glance at the stars and check their path. When she dove again, she said, "Perhaps it's something to do with the Onians. Our people haven't been to war in decades, but it doesn't mean tensions can't rise again."

"Her captors *were* merfolk," Kal replied, thoughtfully. "Those weren't tentacles beneath the fallen rocks. I pray you aren't right, but it's a strong possibility."

Tallora lifted her head above the water once more and this time saw a great ship growing larger on

27

the horizon, illuminated by the eerie light of the blood moon. Past experiences with sailing vessels screamed she ought to dive deeper, but she hesitated a moment—for she knew that flag.

The symbol of the moon, holding the shadow of a skull. With a circle of four-point stars around it, the emblem was the image of the Triage—Solvira's trio of goddesses.

Tallora's heart thumped at the impossible hope, that perhaps Dauriel was there waiting on the deck. Oh, it burned her. Heat rose to her cheeks, fury filling her at her own pathetic reaction. It had been six months—was that not time enough to mourn and move forward?

She blinked, ashamed to feel tears fill her eyes.

"Tallora, are you all right?"

Tallora swallowed her tears, startled when Kal joined her above the waves. "Solviran ship," she replied, finding no sense in denying her sorrow. "Brings back memories."

She recalled the cold, cruel stares of the sailors when she'd been ripped from the sea but clung to those tender, final days aboard the ship with Dauriel, when they'd made love and laughed and watched the stars, despite knowing it was the end. Tallora stared at the distant ship, trembling until Kal's arms wrapped around her. "They won't take you," he whispered.

"That's not what I'm worried about." She hid her face in his chest nevertheless, fighting to dampen her pointless hope. "Let's go."

Sparing a final glance to the ship, she pulled away, then dove beneath the water, grateful she had the ocean to carry away her brimming tears. At night, she remembered their farewell on the deck of the ship, still tasted that final kiss in her mouth, unable to relinquish its bittersweet touch.

Hours passed. When familiar rocks met their view and lights radiated from a great valley ahead, Tallora knew they had safely arrived.

They dove down into the great city of Stelune, the stone structures of their homes vertically stacked, some built by merfolk hands and others carved into the canyon's cliff face. Tallora knew it all as home and loved it so.

"We should go to see my father first," Kal said, his handsome face twisted with worry. "Even aside from meeting Harbinger, I need to know if my cousin is alive."

Tallora worried for her mother, wondered if she even knew of the accident at the Trenches, but realized Kal was right. "Let's go."

The palace had been built of volcanic rocks, smoothed and polished, revealing grey speckles within the stark black stone. Enchanted globes of light illuminated the castle, and Kal led Tallora forward without hesitation, merely giving the guards a quick nod of acknowledgement.

Tallora had been here before. She recalled the decorated architecture and vertical walkways, the pathway well ingrained into her memory after her first visit—a lifetime ago, it felt like, when she had first returned from Solvira.

Six months ago, she had bowed before the King of the Tortalgan Sea, had spoken her truth, even caught a glimpse of her best friend-to-be listening to her explanation. Her momma had been there, tearful as she'd floated behind. Tallora had spoken of her captivity, of Empress Vahla's wicked intentions, of Moratham's more dubious ones, and of the miraculous pardon of Staella to her captor—who was honorable and trustworthy, or so she swore.

She had told it all—save the mention of her broken heart.

King Merl had told her the cruelest words of all—to say absolutely nothing more about it to anyone: *"You're seen as a hero, but you could be a pariah by tomorrow should you come home spouting stories of goddesses appearing and kind Solviran empresses. Instead, let the bloodlust settle. Then you may speak your truth."*

She had intended to listen, but rumors had spread—some true, some outlandishly false. Every ear in the capital city of Stelune had heard it by the week's end. And Tallora's patience quickly snapped, to hear such terrible things spoken of the woman she so desperately loved.

Now, as she swam at Kal's side, King Merl waited once more in the throne room, visibly surprised to see her. With him was a man Tallora did not know, with hair as fiery red as the blood moon and a tail to match. Though a frown twitched at Merl's lip, any indignation at her presence vanished as soon as he laid eyes on Kal. "Oh, thank Tortalga." He immediately swam forward and embraced his son, genuine relief in his countenance. "When you weren't found at the trenches, we feared the worst."

"Are there any survivors?" Kal asked, but Merl ignored him, instead gesturing to a passing guard.

"Fetch my wife. Tell her that her son has returned." Merl finally released Kal, then looked to Tallora as he said, "There are survivors, but the search continues—Raileigh informed us that you hadn't been found. I can hardly believe it—an earthquake at the Great Fire Trenches!"

Kal quickly shook his head as the second man joined them. "Father, Chemon, it was no natural earthquake. Tallora and I sought refuge in the caves, and at the core we found a witch who claimed she'd caused the earthquake."

The red-haired man—Chemon—and Merl both frowned. "A witch?" Chemon said, and Kal nodded.

30

He told the tale, of Harbinger and her torturers, of her bonds and her story, leaving no detail unsaid. "She couldn't speak of her captors because of a curse, but she could say this much."

And he told them, near verbatim, all that Harbinger had said. Truthfully, Tallora was impressed at his memory, but noticed he withheld any mention of herself—no talk of Silver Fire or Solvira.

"Father, I strongly believe this requires the Tortalgan Sea's assistance. Something bad is happening beneath our very noses, and it presents a risk to the entire sea."

"Clearly," Merl said, anger twisting his otherwise stoic expression. "This witch must be stopped."

"I don't believe she's the danger—"

"She holds the power to destroy the Great Fire Trenches. For all we know, she's a crazed, rambling lunatic."

It wasn't entirely farfetched, as far as Tallora cared to think, but Kal shook his head. "She saved our lives. Tallora and I wouldn't be here if it weren't for her."

"You wouldn't have been beneath the trenches at all if it weren't for her." Merl looked to Chemon, a command conveyed in his curt nod. Chemon left, swimming down the tunnel-like hallway. "Perhaps there is a conspiracy, but I cannot turn a blind eye to this Onian Witch. Do you have any idea where she might've gone?"

Kal shook his head, and Tallora bit her lip to hide her shock at the lie.

She dared to speak. "There was a mural," she said, haunted at the memory of the enormous wall of carvings. "A thousand intertwined tentacles and an eye. It spanned all the way across the trench's core and it felt . . . evil. Do you know what it is?"

Disdain showed in Merl's countenance. "No, I cannot say I do." He returned his attention to Kal. "We can speak of this in private. In the meantime, I shall have a guard escort Tallora home—"

"I'd be more than happy to do it myself," Kal said, and Tallora swore she witnessed a hint of annoyance from her amiable friend. When he swam away, Tallora followed.

Once they'd left the throne room, Kal's countenance paled, shock widening his eyes. "He didn't believe us."

"Who is Chemon?"

"My father's advisor. I've known him my whole life." Kal navigated easily through the winding hallways. "Do you want to go home?"

Tallora nodded and followed when Kal swam away. "If your father's heard of this, my mother likely has too. She needs to know I'm safe. But I want to help. Honestly, Kal, I think if you speak to them without me there, they'll hear you. Your father doesn't like me."

Kal didn't try to argue that point. "Something isn't right about this. My father has never been one to dismiss something like this out of hand—not coming from me. We have our differences, but he's always listened. Chemon, too. He's like an uncle to me."

Tallora thought of the Onian and the shifting hues of her skin, her shark-like teeth and single eye. "I agree there's more to this. But I also can't fault your father for questioning Harbinger. She's something, that's for certain."

Kal's voice quieted as they left the castle, the lights of the city bright and welcoming. "Perhaps. But my heart says that something isn't evil."

Tallora thought of her own heart, jaded and bruised. "You're a good man, Kal. If everyone in the world were like you, we wouldn't be in this situation."

He smiled, his slight blush pooling regret into her stomach. "Thank you."

Tallora returned the smile, though hers was forced. "You're welcome," she said simply, and then said nothing else. Was she leading him on if she truly wished to love him? Yet anytime she let him come close, guilt stirred within her, to know she only longed for what she'd left behind.

Kal filled the silence with idle conversation. Tallora clung to it all the way home.

Chapter IV 🐚

After reassuring her mother that she was in fact alive and, *"no, not bruised or brain damaged; I'm very sure,"* Tallora was fed and helped to bed. Since her return to the Tortalgan Sea, her mother doted more than Tallora appreciated, her soothing tones appropriate for a child and not a grown woman at times, but she indulged.

Her mother worried. Since Tallora's papa's death, their little family of two was all she had, and so when her mother stroked gentle lines across Tallora's face to help her eyes to droop, she indulged it, letting it quiet her thoughts.

Tallora did sleep. She knew she did, because all of a sudden her mother was gone, replaced with tapping on the wall. She sat up, the grated window revealing a shadowy figure who perked up at her movement. *"Tallora!"* a masculine voice whispered, and she knew it well.

"Kal?" Surprised, she swam to the window. There he was, his eyes sunken and grey from exhaustion. She immediately flipped the latch on the window grate. It swung open as she beckoned for him to enter. "Is everything all right?"

Kal swam inside, amiable when Tallora led him through the small, cluttered space and to the bed. "I've spent the last few hours talking to my father. He ..." Kal's head fell into his hands. "I'm sorry. I shouldn't be here. But I didn't know who else to turn to. I ..." He looked up, despondence in his wide eyes. "Tallora, something terrible is happening."

"You can tell me," she said, settling beside him.

Kal did not look to her, but across the room at the mirror. Their faces cast eerie reflections, shadowed and hazy in the false image. "The world is on the cusp of war," he whispered, "and we're about to join them."

Tallora's breath caught, yet she remained silent, waiting for more.

"My father said that since your return, Solvira and Moratham have been going back and forth negotiating a border dispute, but the longer it goes, the hotter their tensions get. And it'll be a bloodbath on both sides—Solvira has the stronger forces, they have the Bringer of War—their army is the greatest in the world, but Moratham has a thousand miles of desert between the border and their capital. Even with Solvira's capability to transport soldiers across the planes, a siege on Moratham's capital would be an endless affair in a dangerous environment. For so long they've been at tentative peace, but your kidnapping has rekindled the wrath between them— that's what my father said. You've become the face of Solvira's wickedness, and Moratham seeks to rally the world against them."

Tallora had heard similar sentiments long ago from Ambassador Amulon, whose good intentions came at a cost, though in the end it had been in her favor.

"They've been in contact with the Tortalgan Sea since your kidnapping and are entreating us for aid . . ." Kal shut his eyes, his sigh pained and heavy. "My father knows of Harbinger. He lied because he would not speak of it in front of you. He didn't want you to know any of this, but I think we could use you—your help, I mean." Tallora's gut churned at that, unsure of his words. "My father claims he knew nothing of Harbinger's torture and capture, but he did admit to sending his people to seek her out. I asked him about whatever weapon he was seeking, but he refused to say anything. Tallora, I don't want a war." He finally looked at her, his large eyes pleading. "I don't want our people to die for someone else's feud. I think you're the key to stopping it."

Apprehension pulsed numbly through her limbs. "What do you mean?"

"My father is due to meet with an envoy from Moratham tomorrow—their ship will arrive in the morning. I want you to be there."

Tallora's blood ran cold at the remark. "You want me to what?"

"My father has already begrudgingly agreed—there's something missing in all of this, and that something is the truth. Moratham speaks cruelly of Solvira and their empress, but you've only ever defended her these past few months. Solvira has attempted to send numerous gifts to my father, but he's refused them. He won't listen to me when I try to say Solvira might not be full of the monsters we thought, but he might listen to Moratham if you speak to them. They were told of your return but seeing you safe at home might soften their hearts."

Once upon a time, Amulon had told Tallora that she was a victim of an unspeakable crime, that the princess' perversions hadn't ruined her and that Morathma would still accept her. "Moratham wasn't in the wrong," Tallora whispered, "but they sorely misunderstood the truth." She had tried to tell Amulon, but she did not know if he'd believed her—though she couldn't fault him. Dauriel had come and slain half his envoy then. A more than valid cause for war, in Tallora's mind. "Kal, the feud between Moratham and Solvira is thousands of years old. I'm worried this is a lost cause."

"At the very least," Kal said, his kind eyes pleading, "your words might convince my father to honorably step away. If the worst comes about and the uplanders go to war, our people wouldn't be destroyed in the middle of it."

"I don't think Dauriel would destroy the sea." Tallora couldn't say it with any confidence, though. Her heart hoped Dauriel's love for her came before politics, but her head said she was only one among thousands. She braced herself, steeling her courage. "But I will go with you."

Kal embraced her, his smile nearly bright enough to burn away her fears. "There's no one better to come with me than you. You'll be a hero, even more than you already are. I'll leave you to sleep, but can I come back in the morning?"

She nodded. "Goodnight, Kal," she said simply, and when he swam to the window, she latched it shut behind him.

Sleep was elusive; thoughts of Moratham taunted her all night long.

Tallora awoke early, despite tossing and turning for most of the night. The sun had not quite risen.

She swam up to the main floor of her home, then dove down to the room beside hers, unsurprised to see her mother already preparing for her day.

Mother turned at her entrance. "Good morning. With any luck, we'll have an easy day at the shop."

"Mom, I need to come in a little late," Tallora whispered, bracing herself for the inevitable worry that would come from her next words. "I—"

"Does this have anything to do with that chattering in your bedroom last night?" Tallora's silence brought severity to her mother's face. "You're an adult woman, and I try to respect your privacy, but I thought we were past the days of you sneaking people into your room at night—"

"No, no, nothing happened." Tallora came closer, her hands fidgeting with the other. "It wasn't like that. Kal came over. He needed to talk to someone. And he's asked me to accompany him to a meeting this morning."

Her mother's eyes narrowed, her frown remaining. "What kind of meeting?"

"I shouldn't say. But it's important."

She watched as Momma shut her eyes and released a pained sigh. Her frown escaped with it, leaving only worry lines upon her aging face. "And when will you be returning?"

"I don't know how long the meeting will be, but I promise I'll come to the shop after."

In her mother's stance, defeat slowly settled, and with it came guilt unparalleled. "I wish you didn't have to be so heroic." Her ensuing smile held no joy. "Do what you have to do. I'll manage without you."

When her mother moved to leave, Tallora quickly caught her, embraced her. There they remained, until her mother whispered, "Be careful."

"I will. There won't be any danger."

Tallora didn't know if that was a lie, but tension escaped her mother's figure, which was a victory on its own. "Good luck. I love you so much."

"I love you too, Momma," Tallora replied, and her mother left.

She settled upon a chair, worry fidgeting her hands, but thankfully didn't have to wait long for Kal to knock on the stone beyond her home. When Tallora joined him, he radiated excitement. "The boat has been spotted. Shouldn't be more than an hour before we speak to them. Are you ready?"

Tallora nodded and followed him away.

A ship laid anchor. It sunk like Tallora's heart.

Were it not for Kal beside her, she might've swam far away. Her blood pulsed cold in her limbs as the small rowboat lowered down from the great ship.

The vessel bore emblems of finery, not yet falling prey to the weathering of time and long journeys. Upon the mast was a flag bearing a minimalist crown and an arc of four-point stars; she had never seen Moratham's symbol and found it made her uneasy.

Tallora froze and nearly sank when she saw who accompanied the envoy.

Ambassador Amulon was not a bad man, and she knew his handsome face well as he stood proudly upon the small boat, hints of blonde scruff marring his typically clean-shaven face. When he met her eye, immutable shock filled his features, but not of displeasure. Merely wonder, and Tallora might've offered a wave were she in better spirits. As it was, though he held some honor, his memory was still tainted in fear.

The small boat touched the water, and two oarsmen rowed the vessel toward their party. Two guards flanked Amulon, though while they were armed, they didn't look threatening—merely there for formality. Instead, Amulon offered a deep bow to King Merl—as deep as he could though he stood far taller on his boat. "King Merl of the Tortalgan Sea, I am honored to once again stand in your presence."

King Merl smiled pleasantly at the greeting. "Always good to see you as well. Your willingness to make this journey speaks well of your character."

"I follow the Speaker's will, though I am happy to obey." He looked again to Tallora. "Greetings, Tallora. Forgive me—I'm surprised to see you, though it is good to know for myself you've safely made it home."

"Hello, Amulon," Tallora replied, her shyness dissipating the longer she swam in the man's presence. "It's like I said—all Solvira had to do was return me to the waters of my homeland." She smiled, but it was forced—once upon a time, months ago, Amulon hadn't believed a word from her mouth, deeming her hysterical instead.

"The true victory is your safe return," he said, ever the diplomat.

King Merl swam forward, regal with his crown and sash. "Ambassador, I would like to introduce you to my son, Prince Kalvin." He gestured to Kal, and Amulon nodded politely, his smile sincere. "He has taken an interest in learning the political machinations between our two countries, and I have great faith in his insights on the matters ahead."

"Delightful to meet you, Ambassador," Kal said, ever radiant as he smiled at Amulon.

"Likewise."

To Tallora's horror, Kal gestured for her to come forward. "Ambassador Amulon, I spoke at length to my father last night, and I have reason to believe there is valuable information our two kingdoms may be missing regarding Solvira, so I've brought Tallora here to speak of any pitfalls in our foresight. I believe she is a priceless asset to our continued neutrality with Solvira."

Tallora's stomach twisted, and judging by the sudden forced composure on Amulon's face, the feeling might've been mutual. "I'm genuinely curious to hear what she has to say," Amulon said simply, "though I fear neutrality may be impossible. With due respect to Empress Dauriel, she has entirely cut off any of our attempts to negotiate. She has stated her terms—terms which are entirely unfair to my country—and will not budge unless we bend to her will."

"Tallora believes Solvira would be reasonable to negotiate with," Kal said, though Tallora wished he would shut up, "however if they have outright refused, I suppose I see the issue. Might I ask where the discrepancy lies?"

Amulon glanced at King Merl, who Tallora didn't dare to look at—she sensed an icy mood. "Perhaps Tallora told you, given she was privy to at least one of our meetings—Solvira and Moratham currently hold disagreements regarding where our

40

borders begin and end, and while an agreement was made under the late Empress Vahla's reign, Empress Dauriel has decided she is above her progenitor's laws."

His tone was pleasant, yet it held condemnation. She bit her lip, resisting the urge to speak, when Kal looked to her and said, "She hadn't mentioned it, no. Not in so many words."

Silence settled, and Kal's expectant stare remained. "W-Well," Tallora began, realizing this was, unfortunately, her invitation to speak, "initially it had been agreed upon that Empress Vahla would give me to Moratham in exchange for the border towns, not knowing they intended to return me to the seas. But that meant Dauriel thought I was being sold and came to rescue me."

"And while the end results are the same," Amulon interjected, gesturing to Tallora, "Solvira still did violate our agreement. They have refused to even consider reopening those negotiations, and furthermore refused to apologize for the deaths then-Princess Dauriel caused when she stole Tallora back."

"Might I ask what her new terms are?" Kal said, and Tallora genuinely wondered if he were truly so altruistically innocent or perhaps more devious than she'd previously thought.

Amulon shook his head. "They are irrelevant to the conversations between your father and I—"

"It's the people you stole." The words blurted out of Tallora's mouth before she could stop them, realization striking her in sudden, perfect clarity. "Dauriel—*Empress* Dauriel wants you to return the citizens Moratham stole and sold into slavery."

"I don't know what you're referring to," Amulon said smoothly, no lapse in his smile or pleasantries. "Morathma condones slavery within his borders, yes, but while it is a blessing for those born into that calling, we never force foreigners into those ranks. It is strictly Solvira's business how they deal with the demon-blooded among them."

"But that was what you and Lemhi spoke to Empress Vahla about," Tallora said, fury welling, slow and steady. "In the same meeting you said I was privy too—he confirmed it, and she agreed to turn a blind eye in exchange for a hefty sum of money. Dauriel wouldn't have wanted it to continue—"

"Tallora," Amulon chided, but it sounded far more like he disciplined a small child, "while there is much to say about the radiance your beautiful face brings to this meeting, if you continue to speak lies, I will politely ask you to leave. Perhaps Solvira's influence still clouds your judgement."

The bitter heat of offense coursed through her blood. "Say what you actually mean, *Amulon*—"

"Tallora."

King Merl's voice held curt finality. When she looked back, a sneer upon her lip, his expression wasn't much kinder. "Perhaps you have said enough," he continued, severity narrowing his gaze.

She wanted to scream but managed to swallow it, knowing it would do nothing to endear herself to these men and their conviction of her clouded mind. She turned to Kal, who looked merely perplexed, and said, "Make a list of anything you want to ask me, but I don't know if I'll be much more help."

"Wait," Kal said, and he swam to Merl and Amulon. "Clearly there are some misunderstandings here. Perhaps Solvira won't speak to Moratham, but they might speak to us. Perhaps this can all still be settled peacefully—"

"Kal," Merl said, and though it was more patient than his ire with Tallora, she saw his lip twitch, "your intentions are good, but perhaps we should discuss this later, alone."

"Father—"

Exasperation colored the king's tone. "Kalvin, if you can convince Solvira to speak with us—fine. But we have no way to communicate with them. We certainly can't walk up to Empress Dauriel's door and ask for an audience, given our biological differences.

Perhaps Ambassador Amulon could send a message, but that isn't a direction I wish to take, nor an insult I wish to ask of him. Now, kindly follow Tallora out. Escort her home. You and I shall discuss this later."

Tension settled between them. Kal visibly forced a smile as he nodded. "A pleasure to meet you, Ambassador Amulon. I have not meant any offense."

"None taken," Amulon replied. "I admire your earnest nature. Your father should be proud of your ambition. But I do believe this may be a deeper feud than you realize."

Kal left. Tallora followed, not bothering to offer any farewell of her own.

Tallora swam toward home, but Kal's voice stopped her. "Tallora, hold on."

She looked to him, unable to hide her glower.

"I'm sorry," he said, sincerity in his countenance. "I didn't think ... I had hoped that would go better."

"Kal, Moratham doesn't believe a word I say. Your father doesn't either—this dispelled any doubt about that."

"But I do." Kal let the words linger, and Tallora appreciated them, even if they meant nothing. "I believe you. Can I ask what you meant about Moratham stealing Solviran citizens to be sold as slaves?"

"Precisely what I said," Tallora replied. "And knowing Dauriel, I'm right—it's why she won't negotiate with them. It's as good of an excuse for war as I've ever heard. I only wonder why Solvira hasn't acted yet."

"Be that as it may, this proves my father is also a victim of this misunderstanding, if Moratham won't tell the whole truth. I believe you're our greatest hope for peace. Empress Dauriel will listen to you."

Tallora frowned, her blood suddenly cold. "Excuse me?"

"It's like my father said—if Solvira will agree, he'll meet with them. And who better to ask them than you?"

"Well, as your father also said," Tallora replied, shock dulling her senses, "we can't exactly walk up and knock on the door."

"No, but we know a witch who gave us an open invitation to her home—and if that same witch can destroy the Great Fire Trenches, how trivial would it be for her to help us send a message to Solvira? We don't have to walk up to the door—we simply have to communicate. It doesn't matter how."

The idea was outlandish, yet her heart beat fast, a sudden brimming of tears coming to her eyes at the rush of feeling.

She might see Dauriel. She might hear her voice one more time.

"I . . ." Tallora forced herself to breathe, the hope impossible, even if his plan had merit. "I think your plan might work."

"You'll come with me, won't you? To find the witch?"

Oh Kal . . . She might not love him the way he wanted, but she still could not deny that she adored him. "I will."

"Eel Reef is a few days away. We should leave immediately—we have a whole day ahead of us, and truthfully, I don't look forward to hearing whatever my father has to say tonight. We can't tell anyone we've gone."

"But my mother—"

Kal shook his head. "You can tell her you're leaving, but you can't tell her where you're going. Once my father discovers me missing, she'll be the first person he asks, and you don't want your mother to have to lie to him."

He was right, though she hated it. She gave a slow nod. "I'd prefer to speak to her alone."

"Perfect. I'll go to my home and pack a few supplies—food and such. Perhaps even steal a carriage. I'll meet you at your home?"

She nodded. He embraced her joyfully, laughing as he released her. "Tallora," he continued, "this will work. Trust me."

Tallora believed him, but she struggled to smile, the truth still slowly settling into her bones. When he left, she swam in a daze back to the city proper.

It had been six months, and in all that time Tallora hadn't once considered the possibility of seeing Dauriel again. They had parted knowing it was the end, yet . . .

Her hope remained tentative, but perhaps she might at least hear her voice or see written words by her hand. It should have angered her, how anxiously her beating heart reacted. For months, she'd tried to forget the foreign empress. This would only lead to further heartbreak, but when a smile came to her lips, she couldn't help but think it might all be well in the end.

There remained the task of telling her mother. Tallora entered the shop as a family of patrons exited and found her mother all alone, idly organizing merchandise.

She closed the door behind her, and her momma immediately frowned. "Tallora?"

"I don't want to be overheard," Tallora muttered, demure as she came forward. "Momma, before I say this, just know that everything is fine—at least, it will be. But Kal and I need to go for a few days—"

"What?! *Where?*" Beneath her mother's sudden fury, thinly veiled anguish shone in her wide eyes.

"There's no danger." Tallora's gut twisted at the lie, but she forced a smile. "But it's important. It's life and death for some. But I can't tell you where I'm going, because I can't ask you to lie when you're inevitably questioned about my whereabouts. Kal and I are leaving together, and the crown will come looking."

Mother's face twisted, revealing sorrow. "Tallora, I . . . I suppose I can't argue with 'life or death.' Highly secretive, involving the prince . . ." She shrugged, though her arms crossed over her chest, nails digging into the skin. "I'm sorry. This is sudden and I'm . . . processing. Can you at least give me something? If you don't return, give me a direction to look, I beg you."

"Harbinger," she whispered, and at her mother's confusion, she said more. "If I don't return, ask King Merl what relevance that word has. But don't say it to him, unless you have to."

"I hate this." Tallora saw evidence of tears, watched them seep from her mother's eyes and float away with the sea. "A part of me wishes you were still my little party girl who promised to always be home in time to open the shop. You're different now. You've grown, and that's wonderful. You have a kind and noble heart, but I worry it'll lead you into trouble." *Or worse*, came the unspoken words. Tallora heard them clearly. "Does this involve Solvira?"

Tallora shook her head. Apparently lying was her life now. "I'll tell you everything when I return. I promise."

"When are you leaving?"

"As soon as Kal comes with supplies. I told him I had to say goodbye to you first."

Her mother's lips became a thin line, rapidly losing color. "All right," she said simply. She stole Tallora into her arms, resignation in the gesture. Tallora lingered a moment in her mother's embrace, savoring the safety she felt.

When Tallora pulled away, tears brimmed in her eyes. "I love you."

"I love you too, my brave girl."

Tallora left her, not daring to look back. The entire journey home was spent fighting tears, mostly of guilt.

Once back in the familiar comfort of her bedroom, she packed a small bag of possessions—a comb, a few coins . . .

As her hands skimmed the vanity, she opened the box with her dearest possession—those silly shears, beloved and never used. On impulse, she put them into her bag as well—though it wounded her heart to think of it, they were the closest thing she had to a weapon, should the worst happen.

As she sat on her bed, she thought of Dauriel, heart thumping wildly. They did not know if Harbinger would help, yet even the merest hope of hearing Dauriel's voice if they spoke those thousands of miles away or seeing her summoned image—Tallora knew little of witchcraft, only that it could perform miracles.

And curses.

She shut her eyes, knowing she was foolish to let this drive her. Dauriel was her past. Dauriel was gone. Yet the door she'd shut had swung open, just a hint, revealing bits of light.

There came a knock beside her window. She looked over and saw Kal's smiling face. "Sorry I took so long. My sister spent a good ten minutes interrogating me when she saw me with my pack. I finally had to tell her the truth—that I was going on an adventure with you. By the time she tells my father, we'll be long gone."

Tallora opened the window, grinning as she said, "No carriage, though?"

"It was an idle dream. There was no way I could have escaped with one without drawing the attention of the entire castle." He patted a rather large pack slung over his back. "I brought food though. Do you like camping?"

"No." She smiled as she swam out the window and shut it behind her, praying it stayed given she couldn't reach the latch. "But what's a few days?"

They swam together, avoiding the city until they reached the canyon walls. When Kal offered a hand, she accepted, finding comfort in the gesture.

Tallora prayed this wouldn't mean their deaths.

Chapter V 🐚

Camping was, overall, refreshingly boring.

For three days she slept on banks of sand, alternating shifts with Kal to watch for anything dangerous. But she also swam over brilliant seas of kelp, befriended fish she'd never seen before, and witnessed Kal as adorable as he ever had been. Aside from hand-holding—which he did nearly constantly—he never moved for anything more.

On the third night, she took her watch of the seafloor. But Kal's gentle breathing stole her attention, the soft rise and fall of his sculpted chest. He was unendingly beautiful, and Tallora wondered, if Solvira had never stolen her and her heart, whether she could have given it to him. She loved boys with bright smiles and strong arms and humor, who treated her like gold.

She didn't know what sort of woman she liked. Pretty ones, and that was as much as she might've said in the time before. In her earliest memories, she'd loved their luscious hair, their full lips and eyes veiled from long lashes. But she'd also loved boys and their humor, their strength, the feeling of protection in their embrace. Love had been a silly game, with whirlwind romances and gossip and nights spent giggling between passionate encounters.

Yet in all of that, she'd never felt anything true.

She looked at Kal and so desperately wanted to want him, to hold him and laugh at his jests and let him inside her, figuratively and not. Perhaps she could learn to be content, even if it lacked the burning passion of a lover. It would be a happy existence, of luxury and savoring a cherished friend.

But love was no longer a game. Tallora had felt the stirring of something deeper, a connection of something more important than sex, more than her oft shallow heart had ever known before. The taste of a love she would have died for—and that had nearly died for her.

It had been six months. Longer than they'd even known each other.

She looked away from Kal, knowing a life of happiness and comfort was a mere kiss away. But it felt so wrong to hurt him, to risk breaking his heart if she couldn't commit or her own even if she could.

"I would have made you my empress."

Tallora shut her eyes, her thoughts so loud she wondered how they did not wake him.

The next morning, Kal said they were close. "Eel Reef isn't safe, but my father took me hunting here when I was twelve."

All around, Tallora admired the craggy rock formations, the sickly strands of kelp jutting from the cracks. The sun could not reach them here, and the silence felt weighted, as though any sound might shatter it. "Did he?"

"It's one of my fondest memories," Kal replied wistfully, his smile beaming, ever the charming prince. "It was the first time I'd ever gone hunting, and I was excited to test my skill with a harpoon. In the end, I managed to slay a great white shark, and my father was so proud. I don't think I'd ever been happier in my entire life."

"That's very sweet," Tallora said. "Have you gone hunting since?"

Kal led her expertly through the maze of grey, jutting rocks, occasionally touching her waist to move her along. "A few times. It's one of the few interests we have in common. My father cares for me very much, but we rarely see eye to eye. He seemed thrilled when

I said I wanted to accompany him to the meeting with Amulon, but..." His shoulders slumped, his smile flickering into something sad. "...I think I ruined that."

"I'm sorry to hear."

"He has more of a temper than I do, both in real life and in politics. He does try to see my point of view, but he thinks my reserve is a weakness. Perhaps he's right."

"I don't think that," Tallora replied, though truthfully her mind dwelled on the idea of hunting in a place like this—they'd seen no life for hours. What hid here, among the cold rocks? "I think it's admirable to want peace. There's a time to fight, but not when—"

The ground shook. Rocks shifted; dirt rose. Kal grabbed her when *something* slowly rose from the earth, and though he tried to tug her away, Tallora resisted, realizing it was . . . a cave?

The ground around the rising cave churned like an eel, dusts rising to saturate the water, the rocks cracking and splitting and settling anew. A behemoth of a cave rose before them. It appeared more like a gigantic maw, fifty feet across at least and consuming darkness within. Tallora looked at the jagged rocks above. "I don't like this," she muttered, and beside her, Kal simply nodded, his mouth agape from the pit's grandeur.

"Well," he said, palpably feigning bravado, "anything to stop a war, eh?" Tallora laughed when he puffed out his chest. "Let's go."

"Wait, what? No." Tallora swam back, shaking her head as she surveyed the cave. "This is highly suspicious."

"Harbinger said to not be alarmed when her home appeared." He gestured to the enormous entrance. "I'm forcibly choosing to not be alarmed."

He offered a hand, and Tallora resisted the urge to grumble as she accepted. "But what if it's not actually her home?"

"Then I offer myself as their dinner so they'll let you go," he said with a wink, and although Tallora's self-preservation screamed in protest, they plunged into the depths.

Darkness engulfed them. Tallora could hardly see Kal, much less the space before her. She swam blindly forward, fearful of whatever beings lurked inside an ancient cave—beings other than Harbinger. The eccentric witch would, of course, pick the most inhospitable home in the sea.

Tallora's hand scraped the ceiling. Light flashed. She covered her eyes as the smooth stone she had touched suddenly illuminated, casting the cave in soothing, cerulean light. Shadows shifted, the light staying strong a moment . . . then slowly fading away.

At the last vestige of light, Tallora touched the stone again, marveling as it glowed anew. The strange crystals lay embedded all over the walls and ceiling of the cave, and when Tallora touched the next, it glowed with the power of a small star.

"That's incredible," she whispered.

Childlike wonder shone in Kal's eyes as he touched the stone and watched it radiate light. "It must be magic."

"Whatever it is," Tallora replied, realization settling into her agitated heart, "it comes with the risk of alerting anything that lives here to our presence."

"Harbinger lives here; I'm certain of it." Kal followed as she led, occasionally joining her in tapping the crystals on the ceiling. "I wonder if she has neighbors. Though I'd rather face an ancient eel or megalodon than Moratham any day."

She frowned, but his visage displayed nothing but earnest sincerity. "I'm trying to decide if I agree with that."

"You would know better, though I don't wish to presume." Hesitation colored his handsome features, and Tallora softly shrugged.

"I wouldn't know as much as your father, apparently," Tallora said, and though she didn't mean to sound bitter, it seeped heavily into her words.

Kal slowed his swimming, his attention solely to her. "You said they lied. Who knows what else they've said to endear themselves to my father. Yet, they also agreed to bring you home, when Solvira took you."

Tallora recalled the envoy and their pretty words and grabbing hands. "Amulon can be both an honorable man and a liar for his god—though he was much more inclined to bring me to Moratham than to return me home. He didn't believe me when I said Staella had offered aid—he thought I was 'confused and hysterical.' He claimed there were priests waiting to try and transform me back into a mermaid, but if not I would be welcomed in their country. They implied I . . ." Revulsion filled her, the cold wash of fear still waking her at night. ". . . that I would likely be given to Morathma as a wife." At Kal's appall, she faced him fully, swimming backwards as she softly smiled. "You'll note that I wasn't, and we can thank Dauriel—Princess Dauriel, at the time—for that."

"You mentioned she was dear to you," Kal said, kindness in his voice.

"You've surely heard the rumors, that she violently raped me and forced me to be a concubine." She offered a humorless laugh, the sound echoing off the expansive cave. It seemed to go for miles, yet the walls never narrowed. "It's not true at all, but I know where the rumor stems from—Dauriel gave that very lie to her mother and said no one else could touch me when I was forced to play the part of a courtesan. She saved me, Kal." She smiled unbidden, her heart swelling though it ached. She recalled the night Dauriel stayed up until sunrise to comfort her, the memory bringing pain and joy both. "She risked everything to save me multiple times. I swear, no matter what the people are saying, she isn't my enemy. There's no need to fear her."

"Tell me more about her."

Surprised, Tallora glanced again to Kal, noting the sincerity in his gaze.

"That's the biggest smile I've seen from you in months," he continued, and his fingers interlaced with hers, the gesture confusing given the conversation, but not unappreciated. "Everything you've ever said about Empress Dauriel has been kind. They say she's the most powerful person in the world. Tell me about this supposedly fearsome empress."

"I'd fear her, if I didn't know her," Tallora admitted, recalling their early days. "I certainly did at first. We were placed at odds from the start—she was set to be my keeper, and I was her prisoner. It wasn't until I turned into a human girl that we began a friendship." She'd said as much before, but she spared no details now, her joy radiant as she spoke of watching Dauriel spar with Khastra, of how she insisted Tallora learn to read. "Her body can't bear children, which was why she abdicated her throne initially. She had bravado for miles, but once you looked past that, you saw how much she'd been hurt . . ." She trailed off, recalling the hesitancy and shame in her empress' words. "I shouldn't say more, I'm sorry. This was all very personal to her."

Kal smiled with bright, curious eyes "It's all right. You're processing—strange things will come out."

"What matters is she's frightening because she was raised to be, but she has a good heart. I saw her vulnerable—"

Tallora recalled Dauriel weeping into her breast, having succumbed to a touch she hadn't felt worthy to receive, and clung to the memory of her tender affection.

I would have made you my empress.

She swallowed the rise of emotion, unwilling to cry, not in a cave alone with a boy she wanted to love but could not. ". . . and once you see the soft side of someone like her, it's hard to forget." She shrugged, limp as Kal touched the next crystal. "She is the most complicated person I've ever met. She nearly destroyed my life but risked everything to save me when she realized she'd done me wrong."

"She sounds like a wonderful friend."

Tallora couldn't bear to lie. Instead, she simply nodded.

A shadow passed across them.

Tallora and Kal grabbed each other, both somehow resisting the urge to shriek when the silhouette, illuminated by the crystals beyond, grew steadily larger. It bore no discernible shape, yet they didn't dare to move forward—not until it came close enough for them to see enormous, black pits for eyes and a maw larger than they stood tall.

Terror stilled Tallora's tongue. The beast opened its mouth, revealing endless rows of teeth.

Darting downward, they narrowly avoided the monster's jaws. It resembled a gargantuan shark yet bore the traits of a deep-sea dweller—translucent skin and eyes as large as the moon.

They swam deeper into the cave, Tallora's powerful tail fueled by adrenaline and fear. The light faded. If they were caught in the dark, they'd perish at the mouth of this monster.

She bolted up, skimming the ceiling with her hand as she swam. Kal followed beside her. "What if we hit a dead end?"

"Then we die." She glanced backward—and immediately regretted it, gasping as the shark steadily outswam them.

"Tallora, keep going. I'll lure it—"

"Don't you dare!" she yelled, snatching his hand before he could perform his idiotic feat. They darted down to avoid the snapping jaws of the beast. "There will be no heroic sacrifices here, Kal!"

"Tallora, you're the one who needs to live and talk to—"

The shark turned and dove—they narrowly dodged; the monster hit the wall and groaned, blood seeping from cuts on its nostrils. "We are both surviving this, so help me—!" She shrieked as Kal ripped her away, just in time to avoid being consumed by the beast. They shared a glance and darted away.

The monstrous shadowed neared. Tallora dove toward the wall, likely bruising Kal in the process as he hit the stone—but the monster flinched as it hit an empty space, disoriented as it turned again to attack.

A new silhouette darkened the scene. A voice echoed through the cave. "Now stop that, Kra'tir."

The voice was familiar. By Staella's Grace . . . "Harbinger?"

The shark approached the new figure, docile as an Onian patted the tip of its enormous nose. It was unmistakably Harbinger, with her tentacles and ever shifting hue. Currently, she matched the radiant blue light, though it darkened when Kra'tir's shadow covered her. "I would say you did a good job, but these are my friends," she said, gesturing to Kal and Tallora. "Friends do not eat friends."

Tallora dared to approach, tentatively swimming closer as Harbinger brushed the dust off Kra'tir's nose. On her back was a small blemish, but when Tallora dared swim closer she realized it was a tiny octopus, no larger than her palm. "Thank you."

Harbinger cooed to the gigantic shark, doting on it like a child. "You poor thing. Come home with me." The sweetness in her visage disappeared looked to them. "Well? You came all this way. What do you need?"

There was no ire in her voice, merely a hurried sort of exhaustion. "We need a spell," Kal said politely. "I think you're the best person to speak to about that."

"Likely. Come on, then."

With a hand on the shark, Harbinger continued deeper into the cave. Kal and Tallora shared a quick glance, both of them bursting into nervous chuckles. Tallora's heart still rapidly thumped, but the chances of them living had significantly increased.

Harbinger seemed unhindered by the darkness; it was Tallora who kept lighting the path with crystals. The only sound became the shifting water behind the beast's tail. Grateful for the chance to catch her breath, Tallora kept an eye on Kra'tir, still wary of its massive jaws.

The path suddenly dipped downward, a massive wall before them. Harbinger led them down, and Tallora fought to hide her shock at the gargantuan opening beneath the earth.

Like its own bubble of existence, they appeared in a massive cave, illuminated by those same crystals at every side. Eerie shades of blue and green lit the witch's domain. A cottage of stone in the center was surely her home.

From above, another massive shark swam to join its partner. Tallora shied at the sight of the beast, but Harbinger approached with no fear. "Look at your stupid husband, Kora," Harbinger said, a light 'tsk tsk' to her tone. "Smashed his nose is what he did."

Tallora watched, fascinated at the interaction between the odd creatures. There seemed to be affection between them—not a trait she had witnessed before in sharks—as Kora rubbed its nose along the other's fin. Almost endearing, though Tallora's racing heart had yet to settle.

"Come on, you two," Harbinger said to Tallora and Kal.

Harbinger's home held no blockade at the entrance, but the sharks and the massive cave were perhaps far better deterrents of unwanted guests. Even wanted ones, really, given Harbinger had referred to them as 'friends.' Tallora peeked inside, intrigued at the modest space.

It held all the typical comforts of a single-roomed home though seemed to lack a bed. Shelves filled with ingredients lined the walls—though not ingredients Tallora recognized. A gigantic cauldron, as large as Harbinger herself, remained the one oddity, empty yet radiating something ominous and dark.

"It is cluttered, but I would not change it," Harbinger said, gesturing for them to enter. Her color seemed to settle for the first time, appearing a desaturated shade of purple. "You are starving. I will make food."

Tallora shared a glance with Kal who was, judging by his expression, equally baffled by this unexpected hospitality. They sat themselves in the curved seats, and she wondered if Harbinger had visitors often, given there were three.

The tiny octopus at Harbinger's shoulder detached, its miniscule suckers leaving a small scattering of red pustule marks. It swam to the countertop, its one discernible eye watching Tallora.

This must've been Drak'Thon, Tallora realized—Harbinger's familiar.

The light from beyond suddenly dimmed. A gigantic snout blocked one of the windows, and Tallora heard a great *moan.*

"Right, right—my apologies, Kra'tir." Harbinger stole a jar from the shelves, revealing a gooey poultice within. Tenderly, she rubbed the salve on the revealed parts of his nose through the window, and Tallora swore she saw a faint glow at the contact.

When Harbinger removed her hand, all signs of injury had vanished.

Once she'd returned the poultice to the shelf, Harbinger resumed her flurry in the kitchen. "I was not quite certain when you would arrive, but I did half-prepare dinner. I did not wish to risk any hospitality going to waste."

"Did . . . Onias tell you?" Tallora asked, failing to sound nonchalant.

"Onias is always whispering. Told me you were coming. That, and the cave would not have opened for anyone else."

Tallora spared a glance for the little octopus staring from the counter. "Why?"

"That pretty navy hair. I used a spell. He was allowed passage." Harbinger looked up from what

58

appeared to be an array of raw fish and a knife. "You would have been too, but you would not let me take any hair. Good thing you came with him." She smiled broadly, revealing those eerie teeth. "Onias says you came regarding Solvira. Spoke of rumors of war. Tell me more."

"We're trying to prevent a war," Kal said, his voice startling Tallora—the boy hadn't spoken much. "My father wants to side with Moratham despite not knowing all the facts. Moratham is trying to talk to Solvira, but they refuse to respond. My father is willing to talk to Empress Dauriel and clear the air between Solvira and the Tortalgan Sea, but he has no way to reach her—so I thought we could send a message and arrange that meeting."

"And you want me to do what? Send a pigeon? Enchant their wine so they see visions? I can do many things. We have to make certain it is something to make them listen." Harbinger stared at Tallora directly. "You are friendly with Solvira," she said pointedly, and Tallora's gut clenched. The woman knew. "You should take advantage of that."

"I can write a few Solviran characters, but not full words," Tallora said, shaking her head. "And I can't walk over to the castle and tell them."

"Why not?"

Tallora lifted her pink tail.

"I am offended," Harbinger said as she plated the food before her—whatever it was, it looked delicious. "You think I cannot give you legs? Even for a little while?"

Harbinger brought them food—raw fish, beautifully plated and garnished with some sort of spiced kelp—but Tallora's limbs had suddenly gone numb.

Go to Solvira? Perhaps she might even see . . .

"I-I can't. I shouldn't," she stammered, noting Kal's palpable concern—which faded the moment he took a bite, into elation. She simply stared at the offering, however. "If you know my relationship with Solvira, you know why."

"It is because I know that I know you should go. They would listen. This works in my favor."

"Does it?"

"Oh, to be able to speak." Harbinger held up her arm, revealing the brand—Tallora fought to not show her shock at the fresh, brutal wounds around it. As though a knife had attempted to slice through the layer of skin holding the scars . . . and gone no farther. "I am only saying it is an option," Harbinger said with a shrug. "Otherwise, I will enchant birds."

Tallora looked to Kal, who gently took her hand and gave a reassuring squeeze. "If you're uncomfortable returning to Solvira, I understand. I won't force you to do that. But she has a point. If we can walk in ourselves and talk to them, we have the best chance. They know you; they'll trust you if you say I'm truly the Tortalgan Prince and that my father wants a war."

"You'd be coming?"

"Certainly, if that's what Harbinger can do."

"She can," Harbinger said, having sat at the empty seat beside them. "Same cost, twice over."

Tallora frowned, though when she took a bite of the food, it diminished slightly. By Staella's Grace—it brought her back to years ago, when her father prepared her a birthday dinner of mackerel from the north, dressed in spices she hadn't known the name of . . .

Tallora set down her fork. "The food is delicious," she said, smiling to hide her sudden unrest. "What is it?"

"Flounder," Harbinger said, which was impossible because it was a common fish—Tallora had eaten it scarcely a week ago, "but it is the spice that is special, you see. Very small enchantment. It tastes like a good memory."

Though her smile faltered, Tallora fought to subdue her sudden spike in anxiety. She wondered if she actually felt her eye twitch or if she had imagined it. "You enchanted our food."

"Onias says it is prudent we become friends. Food is the way to become friends."

Tallora's worry hadn't faded a bit, but Kal still happily chewed. He remained cheery even as he asked, "But what is the cost? For the spell, I mean."

"Something precious. Something unique. Her voice is a sure bet." She smiled at Tallora, her shark teeth off-putting. "If I cut out your tongue, you will assuredly have legs."

Tallora couldn't even scoff at the impossible notion. "How am I supposed to *tell* Solvira anything if I can't speak?"

"A fair point. Terrible plan. Perhaps your hair—" Harbinger stopped, then stared at the satchel at Tallora's shoulder. "Not your hair. Not quite right."

Hesitant, Tallora withdrew the pair of shears from her pouch, admiring their glossy sheen. Immutably precious; treasured above all. "But why these?"

"Onias wants knowledge. He wants... sentiment. They are not unique, but their meaning is."

Kal watched; she felt his eyes, but bless his heart—he didn't ask. Trembling, she offered them forward, placing them at the center of the table.

"You, however, have nothing on your person," Harbinger said to Kal, pursing her full lips. "But I will take a memory instead."

"What sort of memory?"

"Something sentimental. Something cherished. Without sacrifice, there are no results. Think on it."

Harbinger left them, resuming her whirlpool as she assembled unknown ingredients beside the cauldron. Tallora took another bite but kept her stare on the shears, the impossible notion still settling like dust upon the ocean floor.

She would see Dauriel. But did Dauriel want to see her? It had been six months, and Tallora had been implored to move on. Her own heart was stagnant, but perhaps Dauriel's was not. Perhaps she had moved forward. Perhaps she had even taken a new lover.

Tallora couldn't bear the thought.

"Where did you get those?"

Tallora didn't look at Kal. "They were a parting gift from the empress," she admitted, recalling Dauriel's shy smile, a bit of joy among heartbreak. "A silly jest between us—I cut her hair."

Kal's nod held apprehension; he didn't understand, but Tallora couldn't explain. "I know what I'm going to give Harbinger. If you don't mind . . ." A shadow passed over his features, suddenly downcast. "The story I told you, about going hunting with my father—would you tell it to me again, once the deed is done?"

"Oh, Kal—"

"Saving hundreds of thousands of lives is well worth the cost of one memory," Kal replied, and in his quiet smile shined hope.

Tallora offered a nod. "Of course, I will—"

All light vanished. The cauldron illuminated—rather, the noxious substance within it. A sickly green, foreign and gaseous, cast Harbinger's face in an eerie glow. "Would you look at that? Beautiful."

Tallora watched, wary when Harbinger beckoned for them to come. The witch looked first to Kal, then landed her hand lightly upon his temple—and when she stole it back, there appeared a shimmering bit of light, like liquid gold, in her hands. She let it fall gently into the cauldron—within, the substance became a violent red.

Harbinger then held out her hand to Tallora. She placed the shears on her palm, which the witch unceremoniously tossed into the brew.

It swirled; it churned, the color rapidly shifting from red to a gruesome yellow, viscous now instead of gas.

Harbinger began chanting—wicked words, forbidden from this world. The tongue of Sha'Demoni, of the demons lurking within the shadows—shadows that rose to engulf them with each word.

Kal's arms wrapped protectively around Tallora, both of them floating as near the light as they could, actively avoiding the shifting shadows. Harbinger's eccentricities had become something vicious and dark. Dread evoked from Tallora's very soul, screaming and bidding her to run—

Light flashed. Tallora shrieked. She covered her eyes—but the chanting stopped.

When she dared to peek, the ambience had returned to normal, illuminated from the outside. When she glanced at the window, the sharks swam serenely among the kelp.

Within the cauldron were two gelatinous, florescent red masses. Harbinger stole two empty jars and scooped them inside. "Absolutely beautiful," she cooed. "This will last you a day and a night."

"A day and a night?" Kal asked, his arms still around her; it wasn't unappreciated, given her deafening heartbeat.

"Permanent transfiguration is a godly boon, but I do the best I can." She offered the jars; Tallora placed them into her pouch. "Give me a moment to pack my things."

Kal's hold stiffened. "You're coming?"

"What if something goes wrong?"

The words weren't exactly soothing.

Tallora glanced to the pouch, unsure of whether or not the offering was a gift or curse.

Was it a mistake to see Dauriel? To stand in her presence and plead at her feet? For the world, no. She would save countless lives, should she succeed.

But by Staella's Grace—what of her brutalized heart?

Chapter VI 🐚

Harbinger left her apparent pets behind, escorting only Kal and Tallora back through the gigantic cave.

"You have an incredible home," Tallora said as they swam through the dark. Once again, she and Kal illuminated the cave with the glowing crystals on the ceiling. "I've never seen anything like it."

"Thank you. I stole it from a leviathan."

Tallora's initial response died in her throat. Leviathans were a nightmarish legend, the children of Onias. "You what?"

Harbinger's smile revealed her pointed teeth. "An old enemy of my father, may he rot in his grave. His name was Yu'Erit, the eldest son of Onias. I did not kill him; I simply stole it when he died."

Tallora glanced about the spacious tunnel. This cave could have housed a city. "How big is a child of Onias?"

"Unfathomably."

She said nothing more, yet Tallora felt weight in the word.

Instead, Tallora spoke to Kal, told him the tale he'd lost, and watched his darling eyes grow wide at every word. "You swear? That doesn't sound like my father."

"It's what you told me," she said softly. "I'm sure if you asked him, he'd tell the story too."

It filled the time until they finally left the ominous cave. Enormous grey rocks lay scattered across the scene, no sign of life anywhere.

Tallora said, "It'll be days before we get there. We should return to Stelune for supplies."

"Once again," Harbinger said, taking Kal and Tallora's hands, "I am offended. Will you allow me to escort you?"

That large eye was difficult to read, and her body had turned the same dark, crystal blue of the sea, but Tallora managed to nod, despite the welling anxiety in her stomach.

Harbinger led them to the great shadow of the cave. "Do you understand the world of Sha'Demoni?"

"It's a parallel world, attached to ours," Tallora replied, wary at the question. "Demons live there."

Harbinger tugged them into the shadow. The world disappeared in a blink . . . and reappeared as something new.

The deep blues shifted into shades of grey, the cave becoming an eerie haze—yet still corporeal. She saw no life, heard no sound, simply a vast, endless void of sea, as though they'd stepped into a mirror of nothingness. All the world was monochromatic, save themselves.

Tallora followed warily as Harbinger led. "Explain."

"The shadows hold tiny cracks in the barriers between the worlds," the Onian said. "We share planar space with Sha'Demoni, but their world is broken, stretched thin. A few flicks of your fins here—" She shook her tentacles. "—might cover a few miles in your world. We will be in Solvira in a few hours."

Tallora looked back; the cave was hardly a mound in the distance. Kal's head jerked as he inspected every whisper and twitch—in a silent world, every sound struck like lightning. "My world? Not yours?" Tallora asked, following close by Harbinger.

"I do not consider myself a resident of either," Harbinger replied.

"Who lives here?"

"The leviathans. Children of Onias. The few that are left. But do not worry—the chance of accidentally finding one is small."

Despite the words, Tallora most certainly worried. "Why didn't we phase into Sha'Demoni in your cave? It would have saved us some time."

The smile on Harbinger's face became painted, an etching in a wall instead of sincere. "When in Sha'Demoni, the cave continues beyond my home. I am not brave enough to face what lives there."

Sudden dread filled Tallora's stomach. "What does that mean?"

"It means I am a coward of a witch who does not want to see her master." There was no ire in her voice—merely fact—but Tallora understood the damning implication.

Onias was a god to fear.

"Legends say," Harbinger continued, "to look upon Onias is to forfeit your mind to his void. Legends are true. Even I would lose my sanity and sleep among the lost should I stare into his visage."

"Why would anyone do that?"

"It is possible to fall into his realm by chance—many drowned sailors have lost their minds. But for some, it is a suicide—to live in mindless bliss for eternity and forget your pain and regrets."

The idea was startling, and Tallora's stomach sank to think of her papa, wondered if it might've been a fate he would have chosen.

"I'm not too proud to admit," Kal interjected, swimming up beside Tallora, "that this conversation is scaring me stiff. Can we talk about something else?"

They spoke instead of idle things for hours, of where life in Sha'Demoni actually did live—"*On land, of course. Mostly in Ku'Shya's realm—there's even color there.*"—until the trench became shallow, and Harbinger led them along the edge of a beach.

"There is an inlet leading to a river somewhere around here. It will take us to Neolan. I cannot follow once you have legs, but I will wait in the lake."

"You really know how to navigate your way around," Kal said, his amusement shown by a single, raised eyebrow.

"You live long enough, and maps become arbitrary. Boundaries change all the time. Landmarks do not."

They launched into a rather animated conversation regarding the land and how it differed in Sha'Demoni, Kal's eyes alight with interest and joy. But Tallora ceased to hear it, her mind instead drifting to the impossible future before her.

Return to Solvira.

See Dauriel.

Nerves cramped her stomach. She remembered their final parting, their tearful embrace, and silly, teasing words.

Behind her eyelids, she still saw the silhouette of Dauriel upon the deck gazing down, backdropped by moonlight. Did Dauriel still dwell upon it? Or had she moved on and not stagnated like a fool?

Tallora's mind spoke much too loud.

When they finally reached the river, Tallora said little, unnerved by how narrow the walls were. She loved the open sea, cherished its freedom. This reminded her too much of a cage, as irrational as she knew the sentiment was.

Finally, Harbinger bid them to stop. She took their hands and led them to a particularly dark corner of the shadowed earth—

Tallora shut her eyes—for blindness and the brilliant sun.

Color enriched the world, the browns and greys of the stony floor welcomed, along with the brilliant blue of the sky. Tallora's face broke above the water, the breeze delightful, the water rushing instead of stagnant, opening up into a great lake. Upon the bank were trees and clumps of grass, the earthy scent invigorating after hours of nothingness, and, unmistakable in the distance, was Neolan and the Glass Palace, a shining beacon upon the sky.

Beside her, Kal's jaw dropped. "It's beautiful."

"It is," she whispered, the familiarity something from a dream.

Harbinger joined them, her silver locks clinging to her grinning face. Her eye had lost its glow, perhaps adapting to the bright light, and her skin took on the cerulean blue of the lake. She held up a hand to try and block the sun. "Once you consume the spell, that time tomorrow you will return to your natural form. Be certain to return here by then, lest you become a flopping fish in the street."

Tallora recalled the flaky, itchy feeling of dryness and shuddered. "Thank you, Harbinger."

"You made the sacrifices," Harbinger said, visibly uncomfortable above the water. "The thanks is yours."

Tallora pulled herself onto the lake's edge, her tail balanced on the shore, and watched Kal's arms and shoulders flex as he joined her. Her tail glittered in the sun, her skin turning to pearlescent shades of pink and white and purple.

"I will be here when you return," Harbinger reiterated, her shifting skin turning earthy, like the lake's shore. "I will not leave you stranded."

Hesitant, Tallora withdrew the jars from her pouch. She offered one to Kal, then carefully unscrewed her own, studying the odd gelatin a moment—

Then grimaced and gagged as she consumed it in one swallow.

Pain seared her legs. She recalled the agony of Staella's gift and felt every tear of her scales, every growth within her new limbs. Like a flaming knife, she swore she was cut in two, and Tallora crumpled onto the bank, breathing labored as she resisted tears.

Beside her, Kal fared little better—she had been a fool to not warn him. "It'll be all right, Kal," she managed between gasps. "This is— This is—"

The pain stopped. Tallora glanced down and saw two human legs, lightly scaled at the calves but the shimmering pink disappeared before it reached her knees. She marveled at the dusting of hair on her arms and legs, clinging to the water and glistening in the sun, and twitched her toes, finding them cute.

She watched Kal inspect his new humanoid form, his hair holding its blue sheen, his body hairier than hers but his calves held those same scales. Yet for all his human oddities, it paled to what rested between his legs.

Kal joined her in staring. "It's . . ."

When his voice trailed off, Tallora muttered, ". . . tiny."

"I was going to say 'exposed,' but that too."

"Take a look at mine if you'd like," Tallora said, spreading her legs, unabashed before a fellow merfolk. "It's also tiny."

Not as tiny as his, but she didn't say that out loud.

Tallora realized, in all her time in Solvira, that she'd never seen a naked man. Thank Staella for that, considering the circumstances, but she could only guess if it were typical to be so exposed.

Merfolk genitalia was, of course, hidden behind a sheath of scales, only revealing itself when aroused. This brought up an unfortunate point. "Damn it. We need clothes," Tallora said, all but ignoring Kal's bafflement. She looked to Harbinger. "Any ideas?"

"I will be honest; I forgot that." Harbinger frowned, then joined them on the bank of the river, pulling herself up with ease. Her tentacles became as insect legs, easily supporting her as she approached a nearby tree, while her sleek skin took on the earthen tones around her.

"Why do we need clothes?" Kal asked, joining Tallora as she watched whatever in Onias' Hell Harbinger was about to do.

"Humans aren't naked. It's highly taboo. We'll be exposed like a nerve and possibly arrested for indecency."

Kal looked prepared to object, but then Harbinger clutched at the shadow of the tree—

And dragged it away. There stood a tree with no dark shadow beside it—Harbinger molded it in her hands, stretching it into a scarf. "Wrap this around yourself, Tallora," she said, offering the strange bit of magic.

Tallora stood up, taking a moment to steady herself on her new legs, but found her body remembered it well. She accepted the shadow, surprised it was corporeal. "How?"

"I am a woman of many talents," she said, stealing yet another tree's shadow. "Anything I cannot do, I simply bargain with Onias for—like your legs."

She handed the next one to Kal, who struggled to steady himself on his feet. He stood a few inches taller than Tallora, his lithe frame translating into a human physique quite handsomely.

With Harbinger's help, Kal ended up with an odd sort of confining undergarment around his genitalia, whereas Tallora's makeshift clothing reminded her of something she would have worn as a courtesan, but after struggling to make the shadow scarf cover both her breasts and posterior, Harbinger offered a second and helped to situate them. Though the makeshift dress was frumpy and strange, it kept her from walking around naked in public.

Kal then began adjusting his—to cover his chest. "No, you're fine, Kal," Tallora said. "It's only women's chests that are indecent for the public eye."

"Why?"

"Uplanders are obsessed with tits." She looked to Harbinger, leaving Kal to mentally calculate that bit of odd trivia, and said, "I can't thank you enough."

"You can thank me by succeeding. I do not want this war either." She returned to the river, beckoning for them to go.

70

Tallora stole Kal's wrist, dragging him through the field toward the gates, only releasing him once he'd steadied his pace. "We'll want to buy actual clothes as soon as possible. Hopefully they'll accept the gold in my pouch."

But Kal didn't reply to that. "I don't mean to say," he said slowly, "that there's anything wrong with breasts. They're very nice—both to look at and touch. But . . ." He frowned. "Obsessed?"

"They keep their entire bodies covered, practically. Ladies only show them off during sex or to feed their infants. Men will pay to look at them if you're a lady of the night."

"That's a lot of power."

"It's not." Tallora stopped a moment, the reality of her new body settling in. "My body was something to fear. And it's Vahla's fault—she placed me somewhere, against my will, where entitled men could pay to use me."

She remembered Lemhi. She remembered his touch. Her body chilled.

When Kal placed a gentle hand on her back, she added, "Nothing came of it. As I told you before, Dauriel slandered her reputation to protect me."

As they approached the guards at the gate, there was a split moment of confusion as their eyes fell on her, then they just as quickly looked at Kal, ascertained his build, and said, "Are you two all right?"

"These are magic," Tallora said, gesturing to their clothing. "We're here to buy proper clothes."

"What happened?"

"We went out to fuck by the lakeside," Tallora replied without a slip in her words, "but our clothing ended up swept away by the water."

Thank Staella—Kal quickly hid his appall and gave a quick nod.

The guards let them pass.

The massive gates lifted, revealing the grand city. The dirt road became stone, weaving through a beautiful arrangement of buildings. People populated

71

the street like schools of fish, all going about their own ways with their own missions. When Kal paused to stare, Tallora stole his wrist and dragged him along.

She wasn't familiar with the city, no, but the gargantuan castle in the center was difficult to miss. Tallora wound them through the streets, ignored the stares upon her shadowy clothing and pearlescent coloring—two oddly colored Celestials were less suspicious than one, right?

There was a different sort of stirring in the air, however—a radiant excitement she hadn't felt since Dauriel's coronation. The whole city had celebrated on that blessed day, lining the streets to catch a glimpse of their new empress. Here, she saw people setting up booths and eagerly decorating the streets with lanterns. Tallora didn't know what it meant, but the joy in the air was palpable.

When they happened by a clothier, Tallora marched them inside.

At the front, there stood an aged man before a wooden desk, and behind him were rows and rows of garments, hung up on pegs. The gentleman, his narrowed eyes exacerbated by his wrinkled face, said, "Can I help you?"

Tallora set her pouch on the desk, then pulled out her small pile of Tortalgan coins. "What can we purchase with these?"

The man's eyes went as wide as the coins. "Are these real?"

"I have business contacts by the sea," she said quickly, "and my Solviran coins were lost with my clothing."

The man said they could take anything they'd like.

Half an hour later, Tallora and Kal left the clothier—Kal, unquestionably dashing in his breeches and boots and jerkin, while Tallora felt like her days in the palace again with layers of fabric swishing around her ankles.

That said, Kal couldn't stop adjusting his collar. "It's so confining. It itches."

"I know," she said, trying to recall how to breathe in her corset.

"I like these boots, though," he said as he shook his feet. "Much nicer than walking on stone."

Tallora stepped into the street and gazed up at the castle—much closer now, with how far they'd walked. "We should keep moving."

In the dense crowd, she took his hand as they wove through the streets, amused at his boyish delight at every new thing. His eyes sparkled with wonder as they passed merchants with their wares and townsfolk setting up tents. A subtle gasp left his lips when they came across a group of children playing with a dog, who barked and wagged its tail. "Are they in danger?"

Tallora shook her head. "Not at all. Dogs and humans go together like we do with whales." She released his hand and stepped toward the children. "Pardon me, but my friend here has never met a dog before. He's from far away."

The children, of course, happily led the dog to Kal, and when he tentatively stroked the friendly creature's neck, a smile slowly spread across his handsome face. "I think I like dogs."

As Tallora watched his innocent joy, she wished she might've first seen Solvira as Kal saw it now—as a place of beauty and magnificence instead of fear.

When they continued on their way, Kal walked taller, his smile inescapable. "Can I say something strange?" he said, immune to the stares of the populace—even with Solviran clothing, they were hardly an inconspicuous sight, with Tallora's stark white hair and Kal's blue, and their shimmering skin.

"Of course."

"I'm excited to try the food here."

She laughed, the gates of the castle growing closer. The road stretched straight before them now, though dotted with festive booths—their destination was near. "It's delicious, I can assure you that. Whatever my confinements, once they decided to feed me, I was well fed."

He frowned and said, "I shouldn't be surprised that they starved you, but that's awful."

"It was, yes. But it truly is foam swept away by the sea. I let go of my anger."

He squeezed her hand, but she stole hers back when she finally reached the guards at the gate. The Glass Palace itself spiraled like a shell, various towers reflecting the sunlight across the world. But the two men between them and victory stood firm. "State your business."

"My name is Tallora. I need to speak to Empress Dauriel."

"Everyone needs to speak to Empress Dauriel. What's your title?"

"I . . ." She frowned. "I don't have one, but if you give her my name, she'll see me."

Kal perked up. "For what it's worth, my name is Prince Kalvin, Son of King Merl, heir to the throne of the Tortalgan Sea."

One of the guards took a long look at his legs, his raised eyebrow evidence enough of his thoughts. "Care to show some proof? A royal seal? Fins, perhaps?"

When Kal faltered, Tallora said, "Six months ago, the Solviran Royals kidnapped a mermaid from the sea. That was me." She held out her pearlescent arms, frustration rising at their sneer.

One guard looked to his companion. "She's, what, the fifth mermaid this month?" He looked back to Tallora, perturb in his frown. "You're the first girl who's brought a mermaid prince with her, but you're not the first 'Tallora' who's claimed to be a mermaid."

"I beg your pardon?"

"Get out of here before we arrest you."

Kal, to her horror, stepped forward. "Arrest us, then!" he proclaimed, his arms spreading wide. "Let's see what—"

Tallora pulled him back as the guards brandished their swords. "What are you—"

"Get out," the guard said, all his good humor gone. "Both of you. I won't say it again."

Practically dragging the idiot boy, Tallora didn't stop until they'd reached the street, ignoring the stares of townsfolk as she yelled, "What was that?!"

"If we're arrested, we're taken before the empress to be judged—"

"No, Kal, if we're arrested we're put into *prison*. The empress doesn't deal with prisoners."

"But my father—"

"I say this with all possible respect—Dauriel's kingdom is substantially bigger than the Tortalgan Sea. She doesn't have time for this type of shit."

Discomposure settled onto Kal's chiseled, perfect face. He gazed up at the castle, the ends of his navy hair nearly falling into his eyes. "Then what do we—"

"Tallora?!"

They both turned at the name, and Tallora's heart soared from sudden joy. "Leah!"

Her friend among the courtesans, who had left her position with funds provided by the new empress—Leah had her son with her, sweet Mocum, and the pair of them ran to Tallora.

Tallora immediately embraced her, her dark hair and amber skin familiar and soothing. "By Staella's Grace, I've missed you."

"How is this possible?" Leah pulled away enough to search her face for answers, her own lovely features glowing and filled with joy. "They said you returned to the sea."

"I did. It's a long story, but I'm here to try and prevent a war." She gestured to Kal, and Leah seemed to see him for the first time—her mouth fell slack as if struck. "This is Prince Kalvin of the Tortalgan Sea. Kal, this is Leah and her son, Mocum."

Mocum stared shyly at the scene, but at the mention of his name, he glowed as only children could. "Hi, Mermaid," he said, waving his hand.

Tallora went down to one knee and held out her arms, overjoyed when the boy hugged her. "You may call me 'Tallora,' young man," she said, recalling the boy had never learned her name.

Meanwhile, Tallora witnessed an awkward exchange—Leah, staring at Kal's face when he offered a hand, then suddenly blinking as the spell broke and accepting it, shaking it furiously.

Kal, ever smooth, said, "Any friend of Tallora's is a friend of mine."

At Leah's blush, Tallora released Mocum, realizing her friend was in dire need of assistance. "Oh, well, I'm hardly anyone of note. Not compared to you. You're a prince, after all."

Mocum spoke, as innocent as his five years of life. "Are you a mermaid, too?"

Kal turned at Mocum's question, beaming like the radiant sun. "I am!" He knelt down before the boy, apparently finding comradery. "How did you know?"

As they spoke, Tallora turned to Leah and whispered, "A little flustered?"

Her blush darkened. "Oh stop—how else am I supposed to act in front of a prince?"

"You were always perfectly composed in front of the princess," she said, and she hoped her wink was as obscene as she imagined it to be.

Kal showed off his pearlescent skin, even took off his boot to show his scales. He really was a child, Tallora realized, mirroring Mocum in mannerisms. She looked back to Leah, who was visibly enamored, and fought the urge to roll her eyes. "Leah, we're here to see Empress Dauriel, but the guards don't believe that I'm truly Tallora. Apparently, there have been other mermaids?"

Leah gave a knowing nod, twisting Tallora's stomach. "Don't forget—Dauriel is officially Solvira's most desirable bachelorette, with her money and power, but her proclivity for women is well known. Men don't bother, but the ladies don't have to be attracted to women to be attracted to her title. After you left, there were reports of women claiming to be you for the chance to meet her, apparently convinced she'd be impressed by their lies."

Tallora felt suddenly hot, infuriated at this news. "They pretended to be me to try and meet with her?"

"From the sound of it, she met with the first few, hoping they might truly be you. Now, any women claiming to be mermaids are turned away with no exception."

"So, because a few desperate whores wanted to kiss up to Empress Dauriel, I can't even try to see her?"

Leah's apologetic smile did nothing to quell Tallora's mood. "In her majesty's defense, there were more than a few."

Had imposters come to her claiming to be Dauriel, Tallora knew she would have been furious . . . and heartbroken.

Tallora cast her gaze to the stunning palace, the beacon of hope now a lost dream. "Then how do I convince them? People will die if I don't meet with her."

"You don't. You ask me nicely to sneak you inside."

Leah smiled, and Tallora nearly shrieked for joy. "You beautiful, sneaky courtesan, you." She hugged her, unable to contain it. "Kal, Leah can help us."

Kal glanced up, apparently comparing toes with Mocum, who had also removed his shoe. "She can?"

"She knows every secret passageway in the castle." Tallora finally pulled away, matching Leah's blush. "You're saving countless lives. I can't thank you enough."

"You're my friend. And as I've said before—it's because of you I can live the life I have now." She gazed fondly at Mocum, though her stare slipped a moment to Kal. "Mocum, darling, put your shoe on. We need to help our mermaid friends."

Kal obeyed as well.

Chapter VII 🐚

Leah brought Mocum, which Tallora thought was odd.

But given the ease with which they casually walked around the side, pressed a false wall, and appeared in a garden, Tallora realized this was hardly risky at all.

The gardens were a spectacle, filled with bushes, statues of animals, fountains, and a delightful, grassy path beneath their feet. The trees had turned orange, to Tallora's surprise, and she watched as a few leaves blew away in the chilly breeze. Kal stared at the plants, visibly enamored with their unique beauty, but Leah forged onward, only occasionally glancing back to check for guards.

When they reached the wall of the castle itself, she knocked her fist upon one of the countless bricks. She held her ear to the stone as she slowly moved her hand, testing each boulder.

She pressed one. The wall slid open. "Quickly," she said, ushering them inside. "There aren't supposed to be guards here at this hour, but no sense in risking it."

When the door closed, darkness drenched the scene. "Everyone hold hands," Leah whispered. "I can lead us through."

Tallora grabbed Kal's and Leah's, then deliberately placed said hands in the other, wondering if Leah's blush would burn bright enough to light their way. She grabbed Mocum's free hand, and his mother led them through the cold, hidden walls of the castle.

An upward slope—Tallora's thighs were new and quickly began burning. But they forged onward in silence.

Time was elusive in darkness, reminding Tallora of the ocean depths. But when Leah suddenly released their hands, she instinctively covered her eyes, prepared for a blinding flash of light.

Leah pushed on the wall, and the light filtered in. It rolled aside with ease—still well used—and Tallora stepped into a memory from a dream.

Here she had lived, for a time—the courtesans' wing, with its couches and many doors, and even a few women lounging about and giggling amongst themselves. They all turned at their entrance, and the few Tallora recognized gasped.

One approached, an older woman Tallora knew and loved. "Mithal," she said as the elven woman embraced her.

Lady Mithal Redwood ruled this small domain, and everything about her spoke of elegance and grace. Tallora didn't know how an elf had come to work here, but the older woman had been a support and a friend. "By Sol Kareena's Light, Mermaid—what are you doing here?" Mithal pulled away enough to stare at her, her sharp features unmarred by her confusion. "You were returned home."

"I was, but I'm here to speak to Dauriel. The guards wouldn't let us in, but Leah was kind enough to help."

Mithal embraced Leah as well, and Tallora grew restless at the time. "I want to speak to all of you later," she said, gesturing to Kal, "but time is short. We must find the empress."

"Check the throne room," she heard as she left.

There were no guards at the door, either for the time of day or for lack of foreign guests—or perhaps simply different rules beneath Dauriel's regime. Tallora glanced around the familiar hallway, her feet guiding her along a path she knew from memory.

"It's beautiful," Kal said softly, and Tallora agreed, the walls decorated with tapestries and rich artwork, illuminated by sunlight cast through the expansive windows.

"We can ask for a tour of their libraries, if there's time," she replied, thinking back to the great dragon skeleton and all the relics surrounding it. "This place is amazing—"

"Hold! Who are you?"

They turned at the gruff voice, a set of armored guards rapidly approaching. "I'm Tallora, the mermaid. I'm here to see—"

"Where are your papers?"

Tallora frowned, cautiously stepping away. "I don't have any. But I'm—"

"Arrest them."

Tallora grabbed Kal's hand, silently cursing. "Run."

She and Kal bolted through the halls, significantly faster than the set of armor-laded men. Still, the steps echoed behind, never quite fading. *"Trespassers! Arrest them!"*

More footsteps clattered through the hallways. Kal, rather unhelpfully, said, "I thought you knew them."

"Not all of them."

They sprinted down a long hallway. A set of guards appeared before them, rounding the corner. Tallora wrenched Kal to the side, down a new path.

She couldn't say how many guards followed by this point, only that they were royally fucked if caught. "My name is Tallora!" she yelled, glancing back a moment to see if they heard. They rounded a corner. "This is Prince Kalvin of the Tortalgan Sea. We have to see Empress Dauriel—"

Pure instinct prevented Tallora from bludgeoning into the enormous person around the corner. She ducked, skidding into the wall on her unsteady feet, nearly knocking over a painting of who appeared to be the God of Death—but steadied it with her elbow, a disheveled mess but still standing.

Kal wasn't so lucky. He smacked right into the armored chest of General Khastra.

81

Tallora balanced herself, realizing Kal was caught by his arms in the general's grip—and then promptly trapped with her forearm around his throat. "Khastra!"

She was far larger than Tallora's memory had allowed. Kal scarcely hit her sternum in height, and the tension in her massive, blue-skinned arms suggested he wouldn't be escaping. Silver tattoos covered her skin, and her horns and tail marked her as a De'Sindai—demon-blooded. "Mermaid?" Khastra said, her glowing eyes scrutinizing as they went from Kal to Tallora.

Relieved, Tallora said, "Khastra, we have to speak to Dauriel immediately—"

"Technically, all supposed mermaids are to be arrested on sight." In her grip, Kal had turned sheet white, but he didn't appear to be suffocating. "Who is this boy and why am I assaulting him?"

"That's Prince Kalvin of the Tortalgan Sea. Like I said, we need to speak to—"

"How are you a human?"

By this time, the guards had arrived, but none would act until the general gave her word. They simply watched as Tallora said, "It's a long story, but we spoke to an Onian witch. Khastra, please, you know who I am."

"Guards, leave. I can handle this." They filtered off, obedient to their general's word. Khastra, well over eight feet tall, spared a glance for Kal, who had utterly frozen. "I do know who you are."

Khastra had been a friend of sorts, but Tallora also knew her fearsome devotion to the law. "You can't arrest us; we're not 'supposed' merfolk. And if I'm recalling the rules correctly, it only specified mer*maids,* so Kal has no crime."

Stoicism remained on Khastra's face, yet the barest hint of a smile threatened to twist her lip. "Except for trespassing."

Tallora pursed her lips, frustration rising. "The spirit of the law says we have no crime."

"Spirit of the law says you should stay in prison for trespassing, but I am not pushing that—"

Khastra's words stopped as she glanced past Tallora, who followed her gaze—and her very soul leapt.

As a princess, Dauriel had cast a presence as wide as the castle walls, her power apparent in her stance and her words. Now she wore clothing to match her new station, the fine, black cloth of her doublet and breeches and cape perfectly fitted, subtle elegance in the pendent at her neck and the crown upon her head. Her dark hair was short, maintained as Tallora had cut it long ago.

But her eyes, those beautiful, soft, silver eyes, matched Tallora's and immediately filled with tears. She covered her mouth; Tallora swore it masked a sob.

Tallora ran past Khastra, who let her go, met in the middle by Dauriel who clung to her like a drowning woman. Six months had passed, but Tallora's skin knew her touch, knew those calluses upon her cheek as Dauriel stroked her face, her expression one of wonder and forced composure. They did not kiss yet, no, but Dauriel trembled as her disbelief faded. "Tallora?"

Tallora nodded, her hand settling to touch Dauriel's hair. "I'm here, Dauriel—" Her words were stolen by Dauriel's embrace, those strong arms gripping her with all the might of a torrential storm upon the rocks. She felt a gentle kiss in her hair and nearly wept, for she had speculated a thousand different things, a thousand different ways for them to meet.

When Dauriel pulled back, Tallora saw only adoration.

"Empress, perhaps you might tell me what to do with these ruffians."

Dauriel did not react to Khastra's brusque words, except to say, still staring into Tallora's eyes,

"They're my guests." She spoke as though in a dream, her words soft and slowed. "For as long as they stay."

Tallora heard footsteps, but she did not dare break the spell between them, the joy in her heart matched only by the temptation of Dauriel's lips—so close, and so brilliantly perfect.

Kal appeared in her peripheral, reminding her to wait a little longer. "Empress Dauriel, my name is Prince Kalvin of the Tortalgan Sea. We've come to discuss something of utmost importance." When his hand settled upon the small of her back, she felt it as acutely as a knife, even with the layers of cloth and a corset between them. Everything in Dauriel's demeanor shifted as she broke their gaze and looked to Kal, sharpness narrowing those silver eyes.

Once, as a small girl, Tallora had wandered too far away from the reef, and in an abyss of open water had stared down a shark. She recalled the horrible dread in her stomach as the predator had surveyed her, her flesh rising in warning. Her father had come, screaming and flailing to scare it away.

Tallora felt that feeling descend once more, though not directed at her.

Dauriel stood as tall as Kal, yet the difference might as well have been miles for how she held herself. When she spared a glance for the foreign hand on Tallora's waist, Tallora fully expected her to tear it off. Instead, Kal straightened his stance and smiled, removing the hand himself.

Dauriel slid her own around Tallora's waist to replace it. "I'll set you up with accommodations suited to your title. We will talk."

Kal's endearing demeanor held an apology. "I don't know that we have time for accommodations—"

Tallora, her attention still on Dauriel, waved off his words. "We can make time for accommodations," she said, feeling like a smitten youth.

"Tallora, we really ought to—"

"Prince Kalvin, is it?" Dauriel's tone now matched her station, imposing and regal, power in every choice word. "An honor to meet you. At Tallora's behest, I will gladly speak with you both over dinner. A royal from the Tortalgan Sea deserves a feast in his name, but as you can see, the lady is exhausted."

Kal had likely never spoken to anyone with a station higher than his own, save his father, and had thus perhaps never been told 'no.' His bafflement might have been adorable, except Dauriel's implications lingered; Tallora's impatience grew. He said, "Are you—?"

"I'm deliriously exhausted," Tallora whispered, but to Dauriel, her presence utterly magnetic.

"Khastra," Dauriel said, "kindly escort Prince Kalvin to our finest guest suite."

"You want me to do what which is not my job?"

Dauriel ignored her protest. "And tell the kitchen to prepare a feast suited for my guests." Her raised eyebrow shot a jolt of excitement down Tallora's spine, even directed at Khastra. Her lip twisted with mischief. "No one is to disturb me. I'll be busy accommodating the lady." Dauriel lowered her voice, her smile softening. "If she'll have me."

"The lady would love nothing more than to be accommodated," Tallora replied, her cheeks radiant and hot.

Dauriel pressed gently on her back, escorting her away. The last Tallora heard was Khastra saying, "Follow me, boy. It is a few hours until dinner."

And once they'd disappeared, once all witnesses had gone, Tallora pressed Dauriel against the walls and kissed her shamelessly, her heart soaring when the empress parted her lips to return the gesture. Each tender motion repaired her broken heart, the scars fading with every moment in her presence. "Oh, Empress..." she whispered, gasping when Dauriel's grip tightened, a threat and a promise all at once, and oh, it excited her so.

"Be careful with that," Dauriel whispered against her mouth. "I'll accommodate you here in the hallway."

Tallora kissed her, finishing with a light nip at her lip. *"Empress,"* she cooed, then giggled when Dauriel grabbed at her skirts, that lurid grin melting any reservations she clung to.

When Dauriel pressed her against the wall, hands skimming her legs beneath her skirts, she whispered, "I warned you."

"Did you, Empress—?" She stopped when Dauriel kissed her neck, giggling at every glowing touch. Dauriel pressed their hips together, visibly reveling in hitching Tallora's leg above her hip. "Not even going to question me before you claim me?" she teased, but Dauriel pulled back at that, her touch lingering; her expression mild.

"I'm not questioning it," she said, tentative joy in her soft eyes. "Not yet—I'm savoring it. I don't want to know how short our time is. I only want to love you for all of it."

Tallora's teasing faded away, the silence between them something sacred. "I love you too."

Dauriel pressed their bodies together again, her groping hands pushing Tallora against a table displaying a vase—which promptly fell to the floor, the metallic echo ignored. They kissed, and Dauriel's hands disappeared beneath Tallora's skirts, hiking down her bloomers and shamelessly gripping her ass. She tossed the bloomers to the floor, her lurid wink sending a shiver down Tallora's spine. Dauriel lowered her head beneath Tallora's skirt and kissed up her thighs, each touch pulling tiny gasps. "Oh, my empress ..."

Dauriel pressed her lips to her cunt, and Tallora faded into the joyous pleasure of her mouth. Oh, her tongue wrote words of wonder, love songs Tallora sighed to feel. Though hidden beneath her dress, Tallora let her hand settle upon Dauriel's head, the fabric tragically preventing her from stroking her hair.

When Dauriel's hand joined her mouth and pushed inside her, Tallora nearly sobbed for relief. For six months, she'd been lonely beyond compare.

For six months, she hadn't fucked either—and by Staella's Grace her body craved it all.

She kept her mouth shut, though each thrust pulled muffled cries from her throat. Dauriel's tongue continued its sweet work, sending jolts of pleasure through Tallora's sensitive body, and when the pressure built and threatened to burst, Tallora covered her mouth to stifle her final moans, her body convulsing.

But what care did she have now if they were discovered? Dauriel was hers, as told by the enamor in her face as she lifted her head from Tallora's skirts, that vicious glint in her eyes as she wiped her mouth on her sleeve. They kissed, and Tallora loved her so.

"Come to my room," Dauriel whispered, the silver in her eyes a ring around a void of black. "I'll have to tear you out of that corset if I want to give those breasts of yours the same treatment—"

"Empress Dauriel—*Mermaid?*"

They looked in tandem to the gentleman rounding the corner. Tallora knew Magister Adrael, recognized his clothing and beard, the scandal apparent on his face at their unquestionably compromising pose. Nothing lay exposed, but her bloomers were still on the ground, Dauriel stood between her legs, and hidden beneath her skirts, her body seeped pleasure. Tallora offered a wave and a cheeky smile.

Dauriel, it seemed, had as little shame as Tallora. "Magister?" she said coolly, her raised eyebrow unquestionably a challenge.

The magister, to his credit, recovered quickly. "Your majesty, you're expected—"

"I'm unexpectedly detained."

"There's time for leisure—"

"Oh, this is work, I assure you." Dauriel offered a wink to Tallora as she bent down to collect her underclothes—an act which brought a fierce blush to Tallora's cheeks. "Tomorrow should be—"

"Need I remind you the repercussions of perceived insults?"

"And need I remind you how precarious your job is, Adrael? Do not reprimand your empress." Dauriel's good humor hung by a thread; Tallora might actually see her temper. "In case you hadn't noticed, someone I dearly love and who I thought I might never see again is here. So kindly do your job and make nice with the people. I'll be in my chambers."

Magister Adrael offered a curt bow and hurried away.

"If it's that important," Tallora said, still seated on the table, "I don't mind waiting—"

"Don't." Dauriel's hand cupped the back of Tallora's head, her thumb stroking soothing lines along her cheek. "There's always something or someone who needs me, but I need this. I need you. Please." Her jaw clenched, and Tallora saw her eyes rim with red. "I know this can't be forever."

"It's not," Tallora whispered, the heartbreak of those words lacerating her own resolve; she swallowed tears.

Dauriel nodded, her lips trembling. "But I intend to keep you by my side for all of it, if you'll let me."

Tallora pressed a light kiss to Dauriel's mouth, the faint whisper of, *"Yes,"* on her lips.

"I don't want to talk about the future yet. I don't want to speak of heartbreak. Let me love you. Then we'll talk."

When Dauriel pulled away and offered a hand instead, Tallora accepted it, her heart soaring when their fingers interlaced. With shaking composure, she teased, "What was it you were saying about my breasts?"

Dauriel smiled, the heartbreak in her eyes steadily fading. In her hand, Tallora's bloomers were held like a badge of honor. "Why don't I show you instead?"

How could Tallora say no to that?

Tallora still didn't understand uplander obsession with breasts, but by Staella's Grace—Dauriel knew what to do with her tongue.

Dauriel's bedroom was as Tallora remembered it, with its massive bed and intricately decorated walls and window—and oh, what a joy it was for her cries fill the space once more.

Tallora lay naked in bed, Dauriel mostly so—her shirt removed, revealing her muscled frame, lithe from years of swordplay. Tallora loved the feeling of her back, every motion of her musculature a delight beneath her hands, but that paled to the lurid glee on Dauriel's face as she kissed her breasts, her neck—oh, she was insatiable, and Tallora adored it so.

When her empress moved inside her once more, one of Tallora's legs above her shoulder, a breast in her mouth, pleasure built in tandem with tears, and when she peaked, she finished with a cry, her body convulsing from orgasm and sobs.

Dauriel held her, kissed her hair as all the loneliness of six months burst forth from her soul. It felt unreal, to be here with the woman she loved. She clung to Dauriel, pressed her face between her empress' exposed breasts, when wetness stained her hair. She looked up and saw evidence of tears on Dauriel's chin. Tallora slid up to level their faces and placed a gentle kiss on her empress' mouth, fighting to suppress her sorrow. "I'm sorry. I didn't mean to cry. . ."

She trailed off at Dauriel's gentle, *"Hush."*

"It's so surreal," Tallora whispered, wiping her eyes with the back of her hand, "to be back here with you."

"How long do we have?"

Now came the time for questions, it seemed. Tallora said, "Tomorrow. I need to be back at the lake by the same time I transformed today. I made a deal with a witch. I . . ." Guilt filled her at the reminder. "I had to give up the shears you gifted me, in exchange for legs."

"Oh, fuck the shears." Dauriel smiled, her tears drying. "I'll give you a thousand of them if it means I get to see you again."

Tallora shook her head, wetness still stinging her eyes. "It was what they represented that mattered. So I don't know if it would work again."

Dauriel kissed her temple, and Tallora savored the feeling. "Who is Kal?" she whispered in her ear.

"Exactly who he said he was—Prince of the Tortalgan Sea."

But Dauriel shook her head. "No. Who is he to you?"

"He's a friend," Tallora replied, bracing herself for her next admittance. "He's a friend I desperately latched onto, thinking he could help me move on from you. But I don't love him. He and I aren't together. And I've never slept with him, I swear."

When Dauriel breathed, Tallora saw the barest hint of smoke leave her mouth. Her forced smile did all it could to look sincere. "I suppose I couldn't have cared if you had."

"Correct." Tallora brought a hand up to stroke those dark, fine locks. "But we didn't, because I could never stop thinking about you."

The tension in Dauriel's smile could have shattered glaciers, but Tallora knew that while it was because of her, it wasn't for her. She leaned in and kissed Dauriel's mouth, lingering until she felt her empress' rigid form soften and melt. "Have you been with no one since I left?" Tallora asked, the words mumbled against her lips.

Dauriel shook her head. "I've been busy. The day to day of ruling an empire doesn't exactly lend itself to courtship. That, and I fell in love with a courtesan with perfect tits. Can't seem to stop thinking about—"

She stopped and laughed at Tallora's teasing smack on her sternum. Tallora smiled, the jest cruel and beloved all at once. "You're a cunt, you know that?"

"You wouldn't love me if I wasn't."

Tallora kissed the smirk off her mouth, giggling when Dauriel clutched her waist and skimmed her hands along her curves. "In all seriousness," Dauriel continued, bitterness staining the words, "a pity you aren't with him. Queen Tallora has a wonderful sound to it. It's what you deserve."

Oh, those words were raw; Tallora still clung to the lingering echo of a promise said long ago—*I would have made you my empress.* "Please stop talking like that." Tallora cupped her face in both hands, forcing their gazes to match. "He's a wonderful person. But he isn't who I want, no matter how hard I may have tried. I love *you*, Dauriel." She pressed their lips together. "I love you," she whispered against them, a pained sigh escaping her when Dauriel touched her again.

Tallora asserted herself, skimming Dauriel's form, relishing the feel of her arms and abdominals. "I know you don't like to be touched, but would you be naked with me?" she whispered, and Dauriel agreed, pulling off her trousers, revealing every glorious piece of her.

Tallora thought her wonderful, loved the rigid contours of her stomach and the subtle femininity of her hips, even the scar between the hipbones—the proof of her struggle to survive. She even dared to touch Dauriel's wrist and stroke a line across the tattooed scars, caressing love upon her empress' darkest moment. "You're so beautiful," Tallora said when her fingers lightly traced along Dauriel's strong thighs. "Is this too much?" When Dauriel shook her head, she added, "Is there a reason you don't like intimate touch?"

Dauriel wouldn't meet her gaze. "If I cared to be introspective, it probably has to do with how possessive I am of my body, but I try to not think about that."

"Won't you tell me, though?" Tallora's hand dared to brush across the scar between her hips, tracing the thin line. "As the one making love to you, I want to understand."

Dauriel stole her hand away, instead bringing it to her lips. She placed a lingering kiss on Tallora's palm. "I suppose I just have to keep something for myself," she whispered, hesitation in her words. "Being naked in front of lovers has never bothered me, but more, I think, out of spite than confidence. I know I'm not beautiful, but—"

"Stop," Tallora said, grateful when she listened. "I've spent the last six months defending Empress Dauriel from slander. I don't care if the slander is coming from Empress Dauriel herself. Because it's not true, and it hurts me to hear you say it. You are so beautiful, Dauriel."

"Not like you are. Not the way I'm supposed to be." Dauriel sat up, and Tallora followed, letting the blanket pool at her waist. She wrapped her arms around Dauriel, listening as she continued speaking. "Growing up, my body was never mine. When I was young, my mother stuffed me into lacy dresses and braided my hair, and the one time I asked to cut it, she laughed in my face and pinched my cheeks, telling me how funny I was. When I began bleeding, she padded my dresses to make me more appealing to the men who came to visit, told me I needed to be comfortable showing more skin because my husband wouldn't want a shy wife. I used to have nightmares about my wedding night and fantasies about slitting my new husband's throat when he tried to touch me."

Dauriel's pose fell, half embracing her own core. "And then I was bedridden for years," she continued, "living in pain from something well beyond my control, and if I wanted to live I had to let them cut me open—and that's not a choice at all. I never wanted children, but it's different when the choice is taken away, even if the answer would have been no." Dauriel's hand fell protectively to the scar between her hips, her eyes growing misty. "I still had to mourn it. But in a fucked-up way, I was grateful, because at least my mother finally shut up about marrying me off to the highest bidder."

Tallora's own heart cracked at the words, her hand coming up to soothe through Dauriel's hair. She had words, yet she did not dare to speak up yet—not when Dauriel spoke such tender, vulnerable things.

Yet Dauriel was silent for a moment, no tears falling though her eyes rimmed red. She touched the scars on her wrist, drawing lines across the raised marks, thinly veiled behind the runic tattoos. "Not long enough ago, I cut my wrists, only to wake up the next morning with something new for others to condemn me for. So why the hell would I trust anyone to touch me?"

Shame suddenly filled her eyes, her gaze meeting Tallora's. "But I hope you don't think it has anything to do with you. You..." Dauriel's voice trailed away, her jaw trembling as she fought for control. "You're perfect. And there's nothing more pleasurable than watching you and hearing you. I-I hope you can accept that. Someday I might be able to try and push beyond it, but I don't believe that day will be soon."

"You silly, worrying thing," Tallora whispered, pulling Dauriel into her chest. The empress clutched her like a rock in a storm, and Tallora would never let her go. "I can reciprocate however you want me to. You're perfect just the way you are, and you're so strong to have survived all that." Dauriel suddenly shuddered, and Tallora's breath caught. "Dauriel?"

The first of Dauriel's sobs evoked a protective instinct from Tallora's soul, a longing to kiss away her loneliness and pain. Tears fell upon her bare chest. "I love you," Tallora said, and then repeated it again . . . and again . . .

She heard, amidst those tragic sobs, a single sentence: *"I've missed you."*

She said nothing to that; merely coaxed Dauriel to lay back in bed. The empress' cries held a heartbreak Tallora knew like her own shadow—for they were the very cries she had wept in moments of weakness, when she knew she was all alone.

But Dauriel's anguish did quell, her breaths shuddering and pained even as her head lay against Tallora's breasts. "Gods, there's no one else like you," Dauriel whispered, despair in the words. "No one else who can actually get me to fucking talk. I think that was the hardest part of you leaving—knowing I would never find another soul I could trust enough to tell all those awful, tender things. For six months, I've been harassed about marriage and finding a match who would bring Solvira a treaty or money—to a woman, my father has assured me. Despite my mother's insistence at picking at that terrible wound, it doesn't actually matter much anymore, given I'm infertile."

Dauriel gripped Tallora tighter, possessive and protective all in the same gesture. "When I say I came to peace with you leaving," she continued, "don't think it doesn't mean I didn't miss you so much it ached. I quietly resolved to be celibate, because the thought of sleeping with anyone when I still so desperately loved you felt like a betrayal to your memory. So perhaps someday I'll marry, but she'll be encouraged to keep her own lovers; I'll never be one of them."

There was a part of Tallora who longed to fix this, to speak tender nothings, to give her empress hope. But her mind was loud, and she wondered ... why? "I have to leave for a little while," she said, then felt Dauriel's arms tighten around her, "but, Dauriel, my dearest empress—why must this be forever? I understand why I had to leave six months ago. But I'm not your prisoner anymore. I'm not a slave to the crown. I've been home for six months, and most of the world has forgotten you and me. And those who haven't can't deny that I returned on my own accord."

Dauriel lifted her head enough to face her, her naked body pressed against her own. "Explain."

"I wish I could say I've been as strong as you, but I don't feel peace. I'm still healing from everything that happened, and missing you—by Staella's Grace, I'm missing you so much. We may not be able to be together every moment, but why not visit? Why not steal moments by the lake? Or you could come visit me by the beach? Perhaps I make a few more deals with witches and stay for longer? I'll even sleep in that gods-awful tank again if it means a few hours with you. Dauriel, if you're willing, I'll do it. I'm offering."

Dauriel's swollen eyes searched her—for a jest, for hesitation, Tallora couldn't say. But she became quiet, then traced her fingers across the slight contours of Tallora's ribs, above her breasts. "I'm not saying no. But there are many factors to consider." She drew a line to her collar bone, where she traced the protruding line of skin. "You'd be putting yourself in danger. Being mistress to the Empress of Solvira is no idle thing, and anyone could put a knife to your throat to try and control me, and I—" Dauriel bite back the words, anguish twisting her features. "I can't think about that. There's a reason we kept our love a secret. You will always be my most cherished person, but I don't think you realize that my heart can't be what guides me. Not with the power I wield."

"I would continue keeping you a secret," Tallora implored, desperate to see light in those soft eyes again. "I could move away from Stelune, to one of the villages nearer to the beach. I would happily live a quiet life if only for the chance to see you again. Everyone says you're the most powerful person in the world; surely there's a way."

Dauriel remained quiet, though a smile ghosted across her lip. "Perhaps there is, though I'll have to think on it."

"You're the empress," Tallora whispered, a teasing lilt in her tone. "Wield your power."

Dauriel laughed despite her drying tears and lifted herself to face her properly, placing a kiss on her cheek. "You want more?"

"You're insatiable," she said, tenderly placing her hand to cup Dauriel's jaw. "But we don't have too, if your heart is too raw."

Dauriel's smile held tragedy. "You always saw right through my bullshit bravado."

"Not true at all. I thought you were a proper asshole when we first met."

Her empress laughed, and it was true and oh so beautiful. They spoke of wistful memories, all the world forgotten as they held each other in their little haven of peace.

They emerged for dinner as two halves of a whole, a single soul broken apart and repaired.

Oh, Dauriel looked dashing in her trousers and cape, nearly as lovely as she was without them. Tallora's heart fluttered with every stolen glance, and perhaps she should have berated herself for falling back under the spell of a woman she'd tried for six months to forget. But now she moved forward with the hope for more. Tallora loved her so.

"I would have made you my empress."

With Dauriel's hand on her waist, Tallora let her empress lead, and everyone they passed gave them deference.

When they reached what Tallora recognized as the private dining hall, a servant left, bowing before Dauriel, but in the few seconds the door remained open, it revealed Kal seated patiently at the table.

The servant moved along, but Dauriel paused and said, "I presume Kal doesn't know about us?"

"No one does," Tallora replied, praying it wasn't cruel to admit.

"Should I keep my hands to myself, then?"

Tallora looked forlornly at the door, discomfort brewing in her gut—the same terrible sensation that arose whenever a relationship had to break apart. This would dash his heart against the rocks.

But he was her friend. She loved him in that different way. She owed him the truth.

"I don't want to hide anything from him. Given that you asked about our relationship, I'm guessing it's apparent he has feelings for me."

"He reminds me of a puppy chasing a carriage."

Tallora didn't know what use a puppy would have for a carriage, but she nodded all the same. "Let me go in first. It would be even crueler for him to figure out the truth on his own."

"You'd tell your empress to wait?" Dauriel replied with a wink, but Tallora couldn't summon the will to smile. She couldn't laugh; her stomach was absolutely sick.

She simply nodded instead, her gaze to Dauriel's neckline until the woman gently brought her chin up. "You're nervous," the empress said, and Tallora couldn't deny it.

"He's a good man. He's been here for me when I had no one, and he respected my wishes when I told him I wasn't ready to be with someone. He's been nothing but loyal and kind to me, and now I'm about to break his heart."

Bitterness laced Dauriel's words. "You don't owe him your love because he gave you kindness."

"I know. But I care for him as a friend, and I don't know how he'll react."

Dauriel's thumb stroked tender lines along her cheek and jaw. "I'll be here, in case you need anything."

Tallora gave a shaky nod, bracing herself for confrontation.

She had never lied to Kal, she told herself as she entered the dining hall alone. She had told him she wasn't ready, that she perhaps might never be. But it hurt all the same, to shatter his hope.

The private dining hall was reserved for distinguished guests—Tallora had only visited once, when she was topless and expected to wait on the ambassadors from Moratham. It would be good to rewrite that experience, even with something as uncomfortable as this. Kal was already seated, and across from him, Khastra lounged in her own chair looking bored. He perked up at her entrance, his smile as bright as sunshine, though it held a curiosity she hadn't seen before. "Tallora, I hope you're feeling rested."

"Well enough," she replied, and then she looked to Khastra. "General Khastra, would you mind giving Kal and I a moment alone?"

Khastra's glowing eyes glanced from Tallora to Kal, eyes narrowed. "I will simply pretend I am not here."

"It's important. Please."

The general frowned, her scrutinizing glare as piercing as the knife at her hip, but she slowly nodded, perhaps confused by Tallora's hesitation. Tallora's gut squirmed, especially when the door echoed at Khastra's exit.

Kal approached. "Tallora, is everything all right?"

"Everything is wonderful," she whispered, and when he offered a hug, she stepped back, shaking her head. "I need to tell you something. And I hope you don't hate me for it, but you have to understand that no one knows this, and no one *can* know this—not if our plan is to work. Your father can't think I'm in cohorts with Solvira; otherwise I'll be branded a traitor, and you'll simply look like a fool. The war will go on, and everything we've done will be in vain."

Kal listened patiently, his pursed lips and handsome brow furrowed. He was beautiful, but Tallora no longer wanted to want him. "But on a more personal note," she said softly, "I've been lying by omission, and I'm sorry. You're the best friend I've ever had, and I would've been lost these six months without you. I love you, and I wish for your sake I could love you the way you want me to, but I don't, and now I don't think I ever can because there's someone else—someone I was never supposed to see again."

Kal gently interrupted, understanding in his gaze. "The empress?"

Tallora nodded, watching his reaction with care.

"I wondered, after seeing you two meet again. It felt like I was intruding, with how you looked at each other. And then I thought she might bite my hand off for touching you."

Silence settled between them. Kal didn't look to be fighting tears, but Tallora saw something akin to disappointment all the same, his radiant aura dimming. "I love her, Kal," she whispered. "I hope you understand why I couldn't tell you."

"I do."

She'd never heard him sound so muted. Tallora's hands fidgeted behind her back, desperately clutching the other. "That's all I needed to say. I had to be certain you heard it from me."

Kal nodded, his stance as stiff as she'd ever seen. "Thank you. It . . . It would have hurt much more, yes."

She longed to hug him, offer him comfort. But it seemed a cruel thing, a paltry substitution for what he couldn't have. In silence, she went to the seat beside where the empress would be—a massive velvet chair once meant for Vahla—and watched as Kal sat himself a ways apart, though the dining hall was only so large.

That's when Dauriel entered, hardly subtle in the somber mood as the double doors rattled against their respective walls. It illustrated every difference between them—Kal, sweet Kal, with his adorable smile and bright, cheerful eyes, perfection embodied in face and physique. And then Dauriel, who strode into the room as a shark seeking blood, nothing darling in her stance—only power. She wasn't beautiful. She wasn't charming. She moved as a tropical storm through her domain, an absolute wonder to behold.

Kal stood in her presence and bowed. "It's a delight to see you again."

Dauriel stopped before him and offered a hand. "Prince Kalvin, I don't believe I properly introduced myself before," she said, voice subdued despite her stare and stance. Kal took her hand, visibly hesitant. "I am, as you know, Dauriel Solviraes, Empress of the Solviran Empire." She released him, and Tallora wondered what he thought, standing at the other end of that piercing stare.

Although Kal's smile lacked its usual light, it held sincerity. "Call me Kal—all my friends do."

"I don't know that we're friends," Dauriel replied, and Tallora's gut clenched at the slight raise of her eyebrow, "but I'm not too proud to give you my thanks. You were a support to Tallora when she most needed one, and I'm indebted to you for that."

"It wasn't a burden," he said, and Tallora watched his hands turn white behind his back, so tightly were they clasped. "She's a wonderful person."

"I've been informed that you know the truth regarding our relationship. My household is well aware, but I'm told it would be best to continue with some secrecy. I would appreciate the promise of your discretion."

Kal nodded. "Has she told you why we're here?"

"Not yet. We'll discuss it over dinner. You wanted privacy, correct? Only my inner council?"

"Yes, please."

Dauriel sat as servants filtered into the room, lounging in her throne like the monarch she was. Classy enough, her display to Kal, though Tallora suspected there was still the intention of establishing dominance—Dauriel was the type.

Magister Adrael soon appeared, his knowing gaze unquestionably condemning when he caught Tallora's eye, but with him came Prince Ilaeri—Dauriel's father.

His colors were subdued compared to what Tallora remembered of him—a man of ostentatious taste and style, with luxurious robes and colorful accents. He'd clearly gained weight, but not in a bad way. Quite the contrary—his face had filled out, as well as lost the perpetual bags beneath his eyes. No fidgeting fingers, but a firm handshake when he offered one to Tallora. "Delightful to see you again," he said, Dauriel's sharp gaze so clearly mirrored in his own.

"Likewise," she replied, confused, and as he sat at the seat beside her, she suspected his wife's death had improved his standard of living.

She recognized Priest Rel of Ilune and Priestess Greyva of Neoma, though she would not say she knew them. With them came a woman Tallora hadn't seen before—ageless and beautiful in a way that suggested immortality, with brilliant golden hair and eyes as soft as starlight. She stopped politely before Tallora and offered a hand. "I have heard good things about you, Tallora. You are a worshipper of Staella, yes?"

Tallora stood up to accept her outstretched hand. "Yes, I am. May I ask your name?"

"Toria of Vale. I am a Priestess of Staella."

"For several generations," Dauriel said as they parted, "there has been no Priestess of Staella in the Solviran Royal Court. I saw that as a grievous oversight."

Tallora smiled as she sat, heart warmed at the thought.

Khastra came behind the servants, who left trays filled with delectable smells and visual delights. Watching Kal study each dish pulled a giggle from Tallora's throat. "The fish is delicious," she said, gesturing to a prepared salmon, "but I also definitely recommend the bread."

Partway through, the empress beckoned for Tallora to come closer. Confused, she obeyed, only to be pulled onto Dauriel's lap, into the large, velvet throne. At the shameless display of affection, Tallora blushed, more so when Dauriel pulled the chair back to the table. "You'll sit with me, won't you?" she whispered, as though Tallora could deny her, as though no one else at the table could obviously hear. Her hand settled at the curve of Tallora's ass, hidden beneath the embroidered tablecloth.

Dauriel was an asshole, but that oddly appealed to Tallora.

Enamored by the protective gesture, she nodded, amused when the servants moved her plate to be closer to Dauriel's. With her free hand, Dauriel offered a piece of decadent smelling meat from her fork, but Tallora stole the utensil and took the bite herself. Dauriel's grin looked more akin to a snake than a woman, with her leering eyes and visible teeth. Tallora wondered, genuinely, what was an act for her company and how much of her truly wanted to devour Tallora here at the table.

Didn't matter. Dauriel was a snake; Tallora was a charmer. "Empress, shouldn't we be discussing business?" she said with a wink, and beneath the table,

Dauriel's hand moved to brush her thigh, stroking light lines as she slowly bunched up her skirt.

"We should," the empress said, her jaw setting, giving no indication of the mischief beneath the tablecloth. The table's attention turned to her. "Kal, you and Tallora came for a purpose, yes? The table is yours. Please, enlighten us regarding this apparent threat."

All eyes turned to Kal. "Empress Dauriel, my people riot in the streets for Solvira's blood," he began, and meanwhile Dauriel's hand touched the bare skin of Tallora's thigh, stroking in gentle, teasing circles. "We came to ask if you would be willing to speak with my father. He has been in contact with Moratham, and I fear they may be misleading him, knowingly or not."

Tallora saw the intrigue shift in Khastra's gaze, watched Ilaeri set down his fork as he pressed his hands together, but lightning coursed through her blood when Dauriel's finger brushed against the sensitive lips of her vulva.

"Do tell," Dauriel said, her finger gently skimming the bud at the top, hardly brushing it as she rubbed. Tallora bit her lip, her hand gripping the back of Dauriel's cloak. "Speak your mind. I give you full immunity—nothing you say will be held against you or Tallora. You have my word, as Empress of Solvira."

Kal told everything—of the witch in the cave, of the conversation with his father, the talk of a secret weapon, and finally of the meeting with Moratham and discussing the border dispute. "I worry Ambassador Amulon is only fueling the miscommunication. Tallora said that some of his words were false."

Dauriel's hand faltered at the name, her touch shifting to Tallora's soft thigh. "I presume your friend is telling the truth," she said softly, yet something dangerous seeped into her tone—oh, that possessive instinct made Tallora weak.

She nodded. It was all she could manage.

103

Kal continued his speech, but though Adrael and the rest looked enthralled by every word, Dauriel kept her gaze to Tallora, the slight lift of her eyebrow raising the unspoken question of, *"Are you all right?"*

Tallora's nod was as subtle as an ocean breeze, and Dauriel's touch returned to the growing wetness between her legs.

She slipped her fingers inside Tallora, and *oh* . . . It took every ounce of her willpower to keep silent.

"Having spoken to Tallora and my father separately, it's increasingly clear this is all based on a misunderstanding. I don't wish for my people to die in a war any more than I'm certain you don't. I'm told you and Moratham have reached an impasse in negotiations but that they're still trying to contact you."

"You are correct," Dauriel replied, her sneer revealing nothing of the mischief beneath the table. "And Tallora's assessment was also correct—I will not budge until they return what they stole."

"Moratham doesn't want a war either if they're willing to speak."

"That, or they're buying themselves time until your people find the weapon they seek." Dauriel's eyes sharpened, but Tallora barely saw it. "You're awfully quick to assume Solvira's motives are pure." The subtle movements of her fingers within Tallora were both agony and bliss. Her grip grew tighter on Dauriel's clothing, the food long forgotten as she rode her silent, subtle pleasure. "Why?"

"Tallora has spoken well of your character. She believes that Solvira will thrive beneath your wisdom and rule, and so do I. I think a future of peace between our kingdoms would serve us both well."

The rest of the table had finished their meal, with Dauriel, Tallora, and Kal as the exceptions. "Thank you." She looked to Tallora, whose gaze had become hazy. "And thank you," she whispered, and while it likely wasn't intended to make Tallora melt, oh, her shy smile nearly made her undone—though perhaps it was simply the fucking. "You always saw the best in me."

Dauriel's fingers withdrew, and Tallora fought a whine. "N-Not always," she managed, fighting a grin when Dauriel discreetly pulled a handkerchief from her pocket to wipe her hand. "I seem to recall telling you how much I hated you many times and meaning it." Her swollen vulva longed for more; the tiniest bit of friction might unravel her completely. "Fortunately, I saw the real you in time."

Dauriel's smile was wicked, the soft silver of her eyes doing nothing to counter it. "Glad I haven't disappointed." She held up a fork to Tallora's lips. "Hungry?"

"Starved," Tallora replied, this time allowing Dauriel to feed her the bite, lips lingering on the utensil. She winked as she chewed.

"What are you proposing precisely, Kal?" Dauriel said.

"I'm proposing you speak to my father and address the misconceptions of Solvira's so-called crimes. If you'd like, the Tortalgan Sea could even serve as a messenger between you and Moratham—a mediator. My father has already pledged to them, but I don't wish to make an enemy of Solvira."

Dauriel's raised eyebrow spoke volumes, and Tallora felt her stomach drop, despite her pulsing pleasure. "Are you asking me to speak to your father in person?"

"Not necessarily, though that might endear him to you. We could even have all three of our kingdoms meet and mediate a discussion, if you think that would increase the chance for peace."

Dauriel handed the fork to Tallora to feed herself, then fell silent. She looked to her father, the unspoken words between them impossible to decipher. When she placed her stare to the ceiling, her grip on Tallora's dress tightened. "My council and I will discuss this in private."

"Empress Dauriel, thank you," Kal said, his smile utterly radiant. "Perhaps we could even have Tallora be there to clear any final misconceptions. Forgive me if this is out of bounds, but perhaps the relationship between the two of you is the missing piece—if Moratham knows that there's genuine love between you two, perhaps they will finally release their grudge."

"That's a rather presumptuous statement," Dauriel said darkly, "given Moratham's laws regarding lovers of the same sex."

Kal's frown might've been endearing, had it not been so pitifully naïve. "Oh. I-I didn't realize."

"You don't know much about your allies, do you." Dauriel's protective grip remained, and Tallora placed a soft hand on her shoulder, willing her to calm.

Thankfully, Khastra interrupted. "You said a witch transformed you two into humans?"

Tallora focused on her food, unwilling to risk being hungry during the night's festivities, as Kal said, "We don't know much about her, though she does own a pair of giant sharks. Her name's Harbinger."

Khastra's frown remained subtle, yet permanently etched. "Harbinger?" she repeated slowly, and again, Kal nodded. "Empress, I insist on joining the party to escort the merfolk back to the lake. I would like to meet this 'Harbinger.'"

Dauriel permitted it. Tallora so desperately wanted to permit Dauriel to do a few more things.

Tallora realized she was the only one left with food before her as Ilaeri said, "We should discuss this sooner than later as a council and have this affair sorted out before our guests leave. Empress, I would be happy to conjure entertainment for them, assuming you can leave your favorite one behind for a few minutes."

Forward, that one. Fortunately, they were in relatively private company—only Kal looked taken aback by the statement.

Well, and Dauriel. "Realistically, no—I can't stand to leave her." Her smile was vicious, but her father's matched. Tallora didn't see a powerplay in the act, however. Something unspoken passed between the father and daughter, and when Dauriel exhaled, Tallora saw literal smoke.

She leaned over to Dauriel's cheek and planted an innocent kiss. "Talk to your council," she whispered. "I'd love to take time to speak to Mithal and Leah—she's the one who let us in here."

When Dauriel faced her, Tallora saw no hint of the powerful empress, but of an exhausted woman, almost pitiful with how her wide, silver eyes showed their disappointment. But it was gone just as quickly— the wicked glint returned, and she said to the rest, "A short meeting. And then I will insist on being left alone for the rest of the night."

When Tallora rose, Dauriel offered her the plate of food. "Please, take this with you," she said softly. "Don't be shy if you need more, or anything else. My home is yours."

Tallora accepted the plate, not particularly hungry but enamored by the sincerity in Dauriel's words. In response, she placed a lingering kiss on Dauriel's mouth, adoring the starry-eyed gaze she received in return. "I'll be waiting."

A servant came to escort them, but Tallora politely insisted on leading them herself.

Chapter VIII 🐚

They found Leah still in the courtesan wing, lively chatting with Mithal. Tallora briefly spotted Mocum in the children's room before being accosted by a warm hug. "Tallora, you are going to tell us why you're here, aren't you?" Leah said, though her eyes kept drifting toward Kal.

"It isn't something we should talk about yet," Tallora replied, unable to help her broad smile. "Too many state secrets."

"This seems to be a habit of yours." Leah's wink conveyed nothing but amusement.

"But I do want to hear all about you," Tallora said, then she looked to Mithal. "And you. It's been six months—what all has happened?"

She spent the evening hearing tales of the mundane, yet every detail filled her with delight. "Empress Dauriel has substantially increased my girls' salaries," Mithal said, and Tallora swore she saw the rare glimmer of approval in her eyes, "and filters their potential clientele much better than her predecessor."

Leah spoke of schooling—first of her own, and then her new career. "I love teaching," she said, the light in her eyes positively gleaming. "And I get to keep a closer watch on Mocum, which gives me peace of mind."

"Educators are esteemed beneath the sea," Kal said, and had Tallora not known him as a man with no airs, she would have presumed he were flattering Leah for how brightly she blushed. "It's the highest calling."

The duo fell into their own little world, discussing the merit of teachers and their influence, and when Tallora caught Mithal's eye, she was grateful the elven woman stared with the same scrutiny as she.

A knock at the door caused no stir or worry, though a servant did enter when bidden. "Pardon, but

Empress Dauriel has requested Tallora come to her chambers."

Tallora bid farewell to her friends, her heart warmed beyond measure. Her stomach fluttered as the servant escorted her, though she knew the halls well.

When she entered the familiar space, Dauriel sat on the edge of her bed, expression stoic at Tallora's entrance—though it softened as she approached.

Tallora grinned at the attention. "You could have joined me," she teased, amused when Dauriel vehemently shook her head.

"Whatever progress we've made, Lady Mithal does not like me," Dauriel replied as she stood up. She stole Tallora into her arms, hugging her as though it had been a hundred years. "And I don't feel comfortable around Leah."

When Dauriel tried to kiss her, Tallora dodged, giggling as she asked, "Why not? She's my friend."

Discomfiture lay in Dauriel's deep blush. "I think you're forgetting I used to pay her for sex."

Tallora hadn't, but the subtle shift in Dauriel's countenance from embarrassment to shame wounded her elated soul. "I remember, but I don't care." She kissed Dauriel's cheek, felt the heat on her face, and added, "I can understand why you'd be uncomfortable around her though." She planted another kiss upon her cheek, adoring the shy smile she received. "How was your meeting?"

Instead of answering, Dauriel kissed her mouth. Tallora did not dodge; instead she succumbed, thrilled for Dauriel to finish what she'd started at dinner. First fell her dress, and then with expert skill, Dauriel tore at her corset strings, letting the garment lay forgotten on the floor.

When they rejoined as one, Tallora savored every motion, though her pleasure quickly peaked. Dauriel kissed her as she finished, and soon she was a disheveled mess upon the bed, breathing fast, body pulsing as her limbs slowly regained feeling. The desperation to feel Dauriel's body had only lulled—not waned—but each encounter, each touch, even the smile on her empress' face steadily healed her broken heart.

Tallora grinned as she melted into the bed sheets. "That was wonderful—"

But Dauriel didn't join her. The empress, shirtless and powerful, yet docile in the calm of the storm of their lovemaking, approached the window instead, toward the luminous moonlight.

She pushed open the floor-length windows and stepped onto the balcony. Tallora sat up, wrapping a blanket around her nude figure as she stepped out to join her.

The night air chilled Tallora's skin, causing bumps to rise along her exposed arms and shoulders, but Dauriel seemed unaffected as she stood by the railing, her lithe muscles illuminated by the celestial lights above. She gazed upon her city far below, saying nothing at Tallora's approach.

When Tallora touched her bicep, Dauriel settled a hand against her waist and pulled her close, into her bare chest. She remained silent, stoic among the stars.

Tallora settled her head against Dauriel's shoulder, watching the lights of the city below—far more brilliant than she'd ever seen. "It's bright tonight," she said idly.

"There's a festival for the commoners." Dauriel spoke as though she gazed a thousand miles away, distant and thoughtful. "The Festival of Flame—it's a Solviran tradition. Royals don't typically attend. Makes the people nervous."

Down beneath the sea, King Merl and his court attended every grand event, their appearance a joyous spectacle. Tallora couldn't fathom living in the shadow of a ruler to fear, but the world still waited to see what Dauriel would become. Solvira was a beautiful kingdom, the largest in the world, but it hadn't been built upon peace.

110

"What's going on in that head of yours?" Tallora asked, though her own melancholy steadily settled—one night of bliss, to sleep at Dauriel's side . . . and then tomorrow she'd return to the sea.

"My council came to no conclusions," Dauriel said simply, "regarding the conflict ahead. Moratham sends weekly letters asking for my attention—they're filled with saccharine bullshit, disregarding my terms. Kal's story gave credence to their true motives—giving your kingdom time."

Tallora placed a lingering kiss at Dauriel's cheek. "I seem to recall a certain princess who vowed to never negotiate with them anyway."

"Yet you've come here asking me to do just that." Her grip upon Tallora's body tightened as the first hints of silver flame rose behind her lips; even her eyes faintly glowed.

Tallora slipped her hand up to touch Dauriel's face. "I need you to breathe." When she took in a breath, Dauriel matched the ensuing exhale, the barest hints of flame escaping from her mouth—the Silver Fire made manifest. "You have a point. I . . ."

Her words trailed off when Dauriel shook her head. "My council doesn't all agree with my personal sentiments," Dauriel said, her stance softening slightly. "They're split on Kal's story. Some would take the peaceful route and clear the air, as he has asked for. Others view this subterfuge as an insult and wish to punish the Tortalgan Sea for betraying Solvira's so-called kindness and scare Moratham into submission—perhaps then they will concede to my terms." Dauriel's sigh revealed smoke but no flame. "It would be wise of me to pray and see if Neoma will speak on the matter."

Tallora pressed closer to Dauriel, feeling unnatural warmth within her, her subtle rage still simmering. "And what do you want?"

Dauriel was silent a few long moments, her stance hardening around Tallora like a shell. "I want to be known as the Solviraes who crushed the Desert Sands into dust—now wouldn't that be a legacy?"

Tallora shivered, though the chill came from within. "But why?" she implored, for something about it wounded her.

"My legacy can never be my children. I won't birth the next in line for the throne, and so I will die as a footnote in the history books—the empress who relinquished her crown to her brother and lived a life of obscurity in this damned castle. Shameful. But even if I do choose to keep it, assuming he doesn't have me assassinated, the line of rulers ends at my name and begins anew with his." The intensity of her words hadn't faded, not a glimmer. Tallora swore she felt heat rising beneath her skin. "There are those in my line who die as legends. We speak of some in whispers, lest we blaspheme their names."

"Yes, but most of them were wicked, Dauriel," Tallora said. "You aren't wicked."

"Most, yes. But not all. Some died as heroes. As martyrs. Some lived with the intensity of the sun and died just as brightly. No one speaks of rulers who die peacefully in their beds."

Tallora turned in Dauriel's arms, alarmed at the conviction in her countenance. "Is this how you've spent your whole life? Fantasizing about your death?"

Dauriel frowned as she looked to her, though not in anger. "And what's so wrong with that?"

"Because if all you care about is your death, you'll forget to live." She laid her head upon Dauriel's shoulder, content to hold her, her heart aching for reasons she couldn't articulate in words. "It scares me to hear you speak like that."

The slight twitch of Dauriel's frown revealed the faintest crack in her resolve, something that spoke not of bravado but of . . . pain. "Then I won't speak of it."

Emotion threatened to choke her; Tallora swallowed it down. "That's not what I want. I only want you to know there's more to life than that."

"Not for a ruler of Solvira. Who am I to deny my goddess the power she deserves?"

And myself, came the unspoken words, and Tallora heard them echo across the landscape, a threat and a promise the whole world should fear.

Tallora rested her head against Dauriel's neck, joining her in gazing across the kingdom. "And what if I told you I only ever longed for peace?"

Dauriel's chuckle soothed her agitated soul. "Then I'd say you were Staella reborn upon this realm and think you perfect."

Lips grazed Tallora's hair. "I'd like to think I'm more belligerent than Staella."

"Oh, certainly. But I adore a woman with spite."

Tallora hesitated before her next words, unable to quite summon the breath to sustain them. "You want a war, then?"

Dauriel fell silent, her protective embrace tightening. Tallora savored the touch of her skin. "My council doesn't."

When a kiss brushed her ear, Tallora set aside her fears. Time was so short. Whatever the future, Dauriel was here now. She was a person to be loved. "It's surreal, being here with you."

"I'd cast away any hope of seeing you again," Dauriel said, sorrow in the words.

"I was told that women came, pretending to be me," Tallora replied, recalling Leah's words. "I can imagine that wore you down."

Dauriel's scoff held resentment, her hands tightening their grip. "To put it lightly."

Her tone drove away any impulse for a reply. Tallora suspected it had scarred more than she'd say. "It's been an exciting few days," she said instead. "The reality of seeing you again didn't settle until near the end, which is for the best. Imagining our reunion worried me. I didn't know how you felt about me."

Dauriel's lips grazed her hair. "I love you," she whispered against the snowy locks, "with all my heart."

"I accept that now, but I couldn't have been sad if you had moved on, because it would've meant you'd managed to move forward."

"We already discussed this." Dauriel's grip grew tighter, possessive as she gazed upon her boundless kingdom. "I don't wish to dwell on it. Please."

Tallora nodded against Dauriel's neck, admiring how her own skin shimmered in the moon's light, the pearlescent hues illuminate. "I'd like to ask something, then. There's something you said that's haunted me these past six months. Words that woke me in the night in tears, more than once." She swallowed her nerves, daring to utter the sacred words. "You said, before I left you, that you would have made me your empress. I know you meant it then." She turned her gaze toward Dauriel, whose lips held a tentative smile. "Do you mean it now?"

No hesitation. "A thousand times, yes."

Slowly, their lips touched, meeting for an impassioned, joyous union. Tallora savored each motion, the kiss holding all the weight of those beautiful words.

When Dauriel pulled back, she whispered, "I despise secrecy, but I could be content to visit you by the sea and have you spend a day at a time at my castle. Perhaps if I leave my throne it could be as we once dreamed after all—that we could find a beach and make a life in between land and sea. There are countless risks, but having you here . . . selfishly, it has broken my heart as much as healed it, and to lose you again is unbearable. If you wanted . . ." She held Tallora's gaze with those enthralling silver eyes, soft and earnest. "If you wanted to stay forever, I could find a way."

Forever? The word settled like a weight in Tallora's stomach—not unpleasant, not nauseating, but different.

"There are witches who can perform all manner of miracles," Dauriel continued, light steadily filling her eyes. "Perhaps your Onian couldn't make a permanent change, but I could find and pay one who could. You could stay. You could be mine. You could be Empress Consort Tallora Solviraes, my wife."

The words burned Tallora's ears, as well as her cheeks. Blushing, she fought a smile, the manifestation of a dream she'd lost suddenly offered on a platter of silver. "Dauriel—"

But Dauriel shook her head. "I don't want you to answer tonight. I want you to be sure." She placed a chaste kiss upon Tallora's forehead, bringing her hand up to stroke the locks of hair around it. "But the offer remains," she whispered, "should you decide I'm worth giving up the ocean for."

She spoke with such finality, yet Tallora couldn't help but smile, her eyes surely glistening as she blinked away tears. "I'll think on it, you beautiful sap." She giggled when Dauriel grinned, and it was all she could do to not burst into tears. "I love you."

Their lips met again, and they stood as a united pair, blessed by the moon's light, when she heard the gentle whisper of, *"You are the love of my life."*

It was impossible to not feel cherished in that perfect embrace. Tallora's head fell against Dauriel's shoulder, tired but unwilling to succumb to sleep—not yet. Fingers slipped into Tallora's hair, softly stroking her scalp as Dauriel's head rested upon hers.

The outside world felt so far away, until Dauriel spoke. "Khastra seemed very interested in that witch you found."

Tallora's hand slipped up Dauriel's chest, between her breasts, and looped around her neck. "Harbinger is an interesting character. Kal trusts her. I don't, but she hasn't betrayed us yet."

"Personally, I'm curious about this weapon your people promised to deliver to Moratham," Dauriel said idly, her gaze a thousand miles away. "Tell me more."

"I don't know anything about it, except for what Harbinger has said. We found her in the core of the Great Fire Trenches. She was tied up and tortured next to a pit of lava that somehow didn't boil us to death. And there was a mural—a massive mural—that's haunted me ever since."

"Mural?"

Tallora nodded, unsettled at the memory. "An enormous eye," she mused, the words an ominous whisper on the wind, "and a mass of tentacles. It looked familiar somehow, but that doesn't make sense."

When Dauriel said nothing, Tallora returned her attention to her countenance, noting the deep frown on her face. "Yu'Khrall," she finally whispered.

"I beg your pardon?"

"I know where you saw that picture," Dauriel replied, intrigue replacing her frown. Excitement seeped into her words. "Put on your dress. I have something to show you."

Tallora obeyed, letting Dauriel lead her back inside. Despite the odd anxiety in her heart, she stopped, breathless as she watched her lover dress, adoring every motion of Dauriel's back muscles as she slipped into her shirt. Oh, she was gorgeous, in her powerful, different way. Enamored, Tallora made an effort to dress slowly, reveling in Dauriel's stare upon her figure, though she knew it came with the risk of being ravished yet another time . . . Her exhausted body wouldn't complain. Time was so short, even with the enticing offer of a future together. Tallora wanted every moment to matter.

"Would you mind?" Tallora said, holding the corset to her body, adoring her lover's ensuing touch.

When they'd finished dressing, Dauriel offered a hand, and there was joy unparalleled in intertwining their fingers. As they traversed the hallways, Tallora asked, "Where are we going?"

"The library, to the Hall of Relics. Where you saw the dragon skeleton."

116

Tallora nodded, recalling her revulsion at the sight.

It was a quick journey down the lift and to the library. Tallora found the sweeping ceilings magical, summoned lights glowing bright in lieu of the sun's light. But Dauriel led her knowingly to a door to the side, revealing a place Tallora remembered from long ago.

Ancient relics stood upon pedestals. Upon the ceiling, expanding impossibly large and high, the skeleton of the dragon Rulira waited, but Dauriel led her to the wall, where Tallora's gut immediately clenched.

There it was, a painting putting into color the same mural deep beneath the sea. Tallora broke away from Dauriel's touch, immediately running to stand before the vast, golden eye. "What is this?"

A hand appeared on her back. "The legend says Yu'Khrall was a son of Onias—a leviathan—who was cursed with an insatiable hunger and sought to consume the denizens of the sea and the land. He fought Ilune, whom he defeated, then began to rampage across the sea. Neoma was called upon to stop him, but she was prevented from slaying him, lest she start a feud with Onias. So she sealed him beneath the ocean, though no one knows where."

"I think I do," Tallora whispered, and Dauriel nodded slowly.

"Neoma did not know what the future would be," Dauriel muttered, "so she left a key to his prison. The story says only the 'Heart of Silver Flame' may free Yu'Khrall."

"She didn't even trust herself with the power," Tallora whispered, wistful at the thought, for the poetic words could mean only one. "She gave the power to Staella."

"Every prison must have a key. Staella has always been known for temperance and wisdom."

"So, Yu'Khrall is the weapon," Tallora said, more a breath than true words.

Dauriel nodded. "But I would say it's a foolhardy endeavor to try and release him."

The words should have soothed her, yet Tallora was left with lingering dread until lips brushed against her hair. Dauriel whispered, "Come back to bed with me?"

Tallora smiled, despite her unease. "I don't know that I'll sleep."

"No?" Dauriel slid her hand from Tallora's back to her waist, pulling her close. "I suppose there are other things we could do."

"You are insatiable," Tallora teased, but to her surprise, Dauriel shook her head.

"While I am incapable of denying you, I didn't mean sex. I wasn't going to go to The Festival of Flame, but..." Dauriel shrugged, her quiet smile positively radiant. "You only have one night in Neolan. May I take you?"

Tallora bit her lip and nodded.

"Come on. We'll find you something warm to wear."

Chapter IX 🐚

Tallora stood at the cusp of a magnificent sea of lights. Her layered dress swished with every step, and a thick shawl over her shoulders kept her warm. But nothing brought more heat than Dauriel's hand stealing her own.

The empress wore nothing to suggest her title, but also nothing to suggest she *wasn't*—no crown or royal pendants, but every piece of her black ensemble spoke of quality, her leather boots shined and new, her doublet perfectly fitted. She had left behind her cape, however, much to Tallora's chagrin.

A path wove between bustling booths filled with merchants selling boutique wares. People laughed, some holding hands with small children who gazed upon the spectacle with the same enamor as Tallora herself. She saw glowing lanterns floating idly in the sky, reminding her of illuminate jellyfish in dark waters. Sorcerers held globes of light, some forming patterns, others juggling. Children giggled uproariously as they held thin sticks with sparking flame at the end handed out by festival patrons, and when Dauriel grabbed one, she breathed a gentle stream of silver flame to ignite the end.

It sparkled like a twinkling star, but instinct said that to touch it would end in tears. Dauriel offered it forward. "Keep it away from your hair."

Tallora accepted, taking great delight in waving it around as the children did, laughing at the lingering visual of light in the patterns she wove.

As they wandered, they came across a clearing filled with a myriad of food and performers, and Tallora watched, transfixed upon one who placed the end of a torch in his mouth—and proceeded to breathe a great burst of flame. She jumped and clung to Dauriel's doublet, eyes half-blinded by the brilliant burst of light. "Is it magic?" she asked Dauriel, who shook her head.

"No. Just a trick. You could learn to do it."

"You're teasing," she replied, utterly taken aback.

Dauriel kissed her shamelessly, their lips pressing together, invisible among the throng of people. As she pulled back, she whispered, "I'm not. You could."

Tallora might've said something saucy, but a sight too strange for words caught her eye. "Dauriel," she whispered, and then she pointed to the other end of a clearing.

There was Kal. And Leah. And sweet Mocum holding his mother's hand. Kal and Leah looked positively delighted at the show, but more intriguing to Tallora was how often their hands brushed together, how easily they laughed in the other's presence. Tallora thought a moment to approach them and tease their apparent flirtation, but . . . no. She turned into Dauriel's side and chose to let them be.

"Isn't that Leah?"

"It is," Tallora affirmed. "Not what I expected, but I'm so happy."

"So am I," Dauriel replied with a wink. "It removes my competition."

Tallora sneered, though it was light-hearted. "It was never a competition."

"True."

The curt reply lingered, and Tallora nearly smacked her on poor Kal's behalf. "You are an arrogant ass."

Dauriel's ensuing grin held a wickedness that made Tallora shiver. "I never pretended not to be. Though you seem to like it."

"I adore it," Tallora cooed, eyes briefly ghosting across Dauriel's lips. "But be nice."

"Anything for you." Dauriel placed a light kiss on her cheek, her ensuing blush as hot as the fire surrounding them. Their fingers intertwined, and Dauriel led her slowly through the crowd. Few gave them mind, and fewer still looked even remotely suspicious of Dauriel's identity. A handful turned away at her approach or ducked into the crowd to clear the path, but to most, she was invisible. She was simply one of them.

"I presume it isn't typical for a royal to sneak out and join a city festival?"

"Not in commoner's garb, no," Dauriel replied. "But the guards know we left, and they'll inform my father if we don't return. He'll quarantine the city to find me."

Tallora merely nodded, because while that realistically seemed like an appropriate response to a missing empress, she couldn't wrap her head around the notion. Any response she might've conjured disappeared as they rounded the corner.

They came across a great statue built crudely from wood, stretching high into the sky. The shape reminded Tallora of an eel, or perhaps the sea snakes in the south, and she watched people pile endless amounts of kindling at its base. "What's that?"

"There's a vibrant and bloody history to this festival. Can I safely assume you don't know it?" When Tallora nodded, she laughed. "This is a snake. The main event of the festival is when they burn it in a great blaze. It should be soon, if you'd like to watch."

"Burn it?" Tallora asked, intrigued at the concept. Beneath the sea, they had no equivalent. "Why, though? Do your people hate snakes?"

Dauriel chuckled, her smile wicked and lovely and all that Tallora adored. "No. But this is a celebration of how the Snake God got his scales."

"You mean Morathma? Is he a snake?"

"No, Morathma is in no way a snake, nor does he have any kind of snake magic. But it's a blaspheme that predates even my empire." Dauriel escorted Tallora forward, closer to the great statue. Before it, a man shouted to gather the masses, but Dauriel kept whispering in Tallora's ear. "There are many accounts of the story—how the Moon stole the Stars from the Desert Sands; I'll tell you the one Khastra told me."

People slowly gathered. Dauriel held Tallora close, lest they be separated in the crowd. "Thousands of years ago, Staella loved Morathma, who sought to be a god. He promised her she would rule by his side as his goddess in the desert, but he was a person of impatience and grand ambition. Many of the angels in that era bore children with mortals. Morathma sought to found a kingdom of worshippers and took many mortal women as his own, because angel women so rarely conceive. He told Staella he loved her, but this was what he must do—though if she bore him a child, it would reign above all."

Tallora watched a torchbearer rise to the pedestal before the snake statue, speaking of The Festival of Flame and its celebration of Neoma and her power. In her ear, Dauriel whispered, "It is said, when Neoma first saw Staella, that they did not meet—they found one another. Neoma was one of the first angels to be proclaimed a god among mortals, also a person of grand ambition, and she loved Staella. But she said nothing of it, and Staella confided in her of her heartbreak, how the one she loved neglected her in his greed for power. When she did finally conceive, the hope of a child fixed nothing—he loved her, but she was not his equal. He never had to say it. It was shown in all he did."

The torchbearer set his flame upon the kindling of the statue, and to watch it felt like a held breath—any moment, and all would erupt. "There is an old song written by Eionei, the Drinking God, that speaks of Staella's heart torn in two—for the one who is powerful and adored but disregards her, and the one who is brash and cold to the world but values her as gold. It's a painful story, painting the heartbreak of a woman falling out of love and miscarrying. When she tried to leave him, it was an insult to his pride as much as his heart—he beat her. He raped her. And he proclaimed that she would be kept locked in a tower in his palace."

Tallora pressed herself against Dauriel, eyes fixated to the kindling. The base of the statue caught flame, steadily consuming the intricate wood. As a creature of the sea, fire was a strange, foreign thing, something to fear, and the hair on her neck stood up in warning. "She escaped," Dauriel continued. "Neoma harbored her, helped to heal her body and heart. They fell in love, and all was well until Morathma came to find her. What ensued, they say, is a battle that spanned both the Angelic Realm and the mortal plane. They meant to kill the other, but in the end, the Silver Fire manifested stronger than it ever had before."

Fire engulfed the wooden statue; around them the people cheered. Tallora froze at the nightmarish visage, the snake's face burning as its stare bore into her, piercing down to her soul. The heat rose, and Tallora felt suddenly suffocated among the dense crowd. But Dauriel stared with vigor upon the burning snake, the wood creaking painfully within, crackling to deafen the onlookers. "Fire consumed him. They say his screams were heard even in Sha'Demoni and all across the mortal realm. He was said to once be the most beautiful of all the angels, but now he was mutilated, irreversibly scarred. He might have died had Staella not intervened, urging Neoma to simply walk away and let him live with his crime and his loss. Some call it a mercy, a second chance—but others say it was the cruelest fate he could have faced."

When Dauriel's words faded, Tallora gazed upon the macabre sight, feeling uneasy amidst the jeering crowd. *Snake God . . .* It was an unbearably cruel name. Yet he was a god, and he had earned his title and fate—blasphemy was the only weapon the common folk had. Still, her stomach twisted in nausea, sick at the meaning, the message, and the mockery, yet that paled to her fear of that great, burning flame.

"Every year," Dauriel said softly, "my people celebrate the day their supreme goddess enacted vengeance for Morathma's horrific crime. Ilune herself is said to have started the festival when she founded Solvira, though she was not born until many centuries later. Solvira is not perfect, but my people are free to live as they will, so long as they harm no one and pay their taxes. Moratham's atrocities trickle down from the top. Slavery is common practice. Women, they claim, are esteemed, but placing someone upon a pedestal and silencing their voice is a cruel fate. And lovers like you and I would be killed if we're lucky." Her grip tightened as she stared upon the burning image, the fire casting her eyes in hellish shades.

Tallora stayed stiff, even when Dauriel placed a kiss in her hair. The heat rose ever higher, and the burning snake slowly became a skeletal nightmare. She felt choked in the crowd, her skin longing for cool, soothing water. "I don't know if I can watch this anymore. I'm sorry."

"Don't be sorry," Dauriel said, her gaze finally torn from the burning statue. Confusion shown in her countenance, as well as concern, but she coaxed them through the thick sea of people nevertheless, unafraid to push aside onlookers.

At the edge of the crowd, Tallora could finally breathe. The burning snake leered behind them, but she leaned into Dauriel's side, facing away.

"Are you all right?" the empress said, and Tallora nodded.

As she took deep, comforting breaths, she managed to collect her thoughts, even as the jeering crowd kept their unruly energy. Behind her, the snake burned, the memory certain to haunt her. "It's morbid," she said, the smell of smoke inescapable, though it no longer choked her. "I'm all right. But I can't imagine Staella condoning this, so I just don't understand."

"Ilune started the festival, and she's not exactly known for kindness. She was not the first to call him *Snake,* but she certainly popularized it."

Tallora pressed into her embrace, grateful for her presence. "I'm also not used to fire," she said, managing to force a smile.

"You have a tender heart, underneath your spite," Dauriel said, enamor in her soft smile. "I admire that. If we embrace the impossible dream of you ruling at my side, it will serve this kingdom well."

To be reminded of the flickering hope of their future threatened to bring tears to Tallora's eyes. She released a stabilizing sigh, pushing away her discomfiture, then brought a gentle hand up to cup Dauriel's cheek. "Dauriel—"

An explosion shook the sky. Tallora screamed as vibrant colors burst across the night's palette. "Dauriel, run!"

But Dauriel did not run, nor did anyone else panic as Tallora did; they cheered too loudly to notice her scream. "It's all right. We're not in danger—"

Another great *boom* reverberated across Tallora's whole body. At Dauriel's gentle coaxing, she looked to the night sky and watched the final vestiges of flame high above fizzle out. "It's part of the celebration," Dauriel said, but she brought a hand to caress Tallora's back nonetheless.

Safe in Dauriel's arms, Tallora watched a third beam of light shoot into the sky and burst into an array of colorful flame. Her panicked heart still raced, but she saw the beauty in its vibrancy, though she reeled at how her body shook with the explosion. "You swear we're safe?"

"Perfectly safe, my love." Still, Dauriel held her close, soothing soft lines across her back. Tallora dared to watch the fourth explosion, finding it less frightening this time, and even managed a small smile at the next.

"Is it magic?"

"No," Dauriel said, and Tallora might've though she jested were it not for the serenity upon her features.

Dauriel loved things of beauty, and Tallora would not deny her a moment of it. Now was not the time for fear, or so Dauriel had said. Instead, Tallora tucked her head against her empress' shoulder and watched the brilliant display, her mind contemplating the day's events. But when her empress laughed at a particularly colorful burst, Tallora forgot all that and simply joined her, finding peace in her joy.

When the blasts of colorful flame quelled, most of the crowd slowly dispersed, leaving the wooden snake to burn. Dauriel held her close, her gaze not upon the remains of the blasphemous statue, but on a far-off tower beyond the clusters of people. "May we stop somewhere before I take you to the castle?"

Tallora nodded against her doublet. "My heart is still racing. I won't sleep yet."

Dauriel's hand left her waist and instead stole her hand as she wove them through the crowds of people, to a quiet side-street. They left the chaos of the festival and instead appeared in a vacant street, shut down for the festivities, save for a familiar temple bearing the symbols of the Triage.

Unity, Tallora recalled, where she and Dauriel had faced intercession all those months ago, and as her empress led her up the steps, anxiety gripped her chest.

They entered unimpeded, for temples were rarely closed, and when the priest on duty saw Dauriel, he bowed. "Empress Dauriel, it is an honor."

"I require a private space," she said in reply— no greeting, nothing polite, but Dauriel had never been known for pleasant airs. When the priest escorted them through the hall, they did not enter the chapel, but an unoccupied room—smaller but still bearing an altar clearly decorated for the Moon Goddess. Open skylights cast celestial light into the room, and a statue of Neoma's likeness stood nearly twice a human's height. Dauriel marched forward, and Tallora was struck by the similarities in their stances, the relentless glints in their eyes. Neoma's statue held a warrior's garb and did not stand in a gesture of welcome; instead, she dared you to approach, the severity of her gaze promising a lashing for wasting her time. Neoma's power outshone the rest; her wrath was endless, her grudges eternal; her kingdom was the largest in the realm.

In the triage of goddesses, one was gentle, one was wicked, and between them, the one who reigned above the rest, was ruthless—not evil, not good, but justice incarnate.

"Have a seat," Dauriel said, escorting Tallora to a pew. "I don't know how your presence will affect this meeting, but please don't be offended if you're asked to leave."

"This isn't about me," Tallora replied, her smile sincere. "And I'm not much of anyone anyway. Neoma has no reason to want to talk to me."

Dauriel kissed her hair, a soft chuckle escaping her throat. "The woman whose word dictated whether the previous empress lived or died? Tallora, she won't ever forget you."

The words were . . . not soothing.

Dauriel stepped toward the statue at the head of the room, a spark of silver light flashing in her hand. Fire rose, and when she placed her palm upon the statue's core, light filled the cracks, spreading from her touch. When Dauriel pulled back, the statue's light continued growing, dispersing throughout her godly figure, ending with her wings—

Which suddenly undulated as though weightless, no longer inhibited by stone.

Nothing else moved. Yet the entire mood shifted, all focus drawn to the statue. Its presence seemed to grow, though it did not move except for the wings and the light.

"Goddess Neoma," Dauriel said, bowing low at the waist. "I request an audience with you this night."

Words echoed across the room—unmistakable, for Tallora had heard them before. *Dauriel Solviraes,* Neoma said, something domineering in her tone, *you brought an interloper.*

"Tallora is as important to me as my crown," Dauriel replied, and the words brought a blush to Tallora's cheeks. "But if it offends you, I can ask her to step out."

We shall see. Speak your mind.

"Tallora presented proof that Moratham has been conspiring with her people against Solvira," Dauriel said, rushing straight to the point, it seemed, but perhaps that was how to best interact with Neoma. "There is evidence that they may be seeking to release the leviathan, Yu'Khrall."

Interesting.

Dauriel paused, perhaps waiting for more. But the word lingered; the empress finally spoke anew. "I seek your guidance. I know what I want, and I know what my council wants, but it is your will I would enact."

I delegated those responsibilities to you when you accepted your crown, Neoma said, severity in her words. As she sat quietly in her chair, Tallora felt them reverberate against her bones. *You know my will. You know my teachings. It is your duty, as my voice upon this earth, to interpret it.*

"I understand this, but—"

But what, Dauriel Solviraes?

128

The reprimand hung in the air like a noose.

Were I the sort to force my will, I would have a Speaker, Neoma continued, her words no less subdued. In her chair, Tallora sunk into the firm cushions. *Solvira's strength comes from its capacity to rule itself, without the constant interference from gods. Self-governance makes for a powerful people, and it is not something the people beneath Morathma's thumb have any understanding of. I am here to be worshipped, but I am not here to rule. Instead, I am here to serve and place those in my charge above myself. It is where true strength lies, Dauriel. I have and will always give you what you need to succeed, but it is your responsibility to act.*

Tallora listened intently, intrigued by the sentiment, but not missing how Dauriel's hands fidgeted behind her back.

We gods of Celestière follow laws, though they are different than yours. Morathma may appear to speak, but he cannot appear to fight, lest I personally retaliate. It is my duty to handle Morathma; it is yours to handle his people.

"Goddess Neoma, I accept that it is wrong, but I am begging to know what you would do if you were me," Dauriel said, and to Tallora's surprise, she sounded ... wounded. "I fear the diverging path ahead. Not because I shy from war or pain, but because ... I ..."

Her words faded. The silence settled with as heavy a presence as Neoma herself.

The voice spoke, startling Tallora—more when it spoke her name. *Tallora, leave us. My next words are for the Empress of Solvira. They are her burden to bear alone.*

Tallora stood, a protective instinct filling her though she dared not fight the great goddess. She did come forward first, however, stealing Dauriel from behind in a quick embrace. "Whatever burdens you must bear alone," she whispered, "you will not *be* alone."

She slipped away; Dauriel did not move or react. Her steps were the only sound as she left the small worship hall, Neoma's light stopping at the doorframe, belligerently unwilling to touch the outside world.

When the door shut, dark hallways surrounded her. A distant sconce flickered on the wall, but Tallora was left isolated among stone. There was no point in eavesdropping, even if she wanted to—if Neoma's light would not touch beyond the bounds of the room, her sound surely wouldn't either.

Tallora idly wandered toward the light, the sconce serving to illuminate a piece of artwork. The image depicted a grand representation of Solvira's Moon Goddess—she stood with all the power of a storm upon the sea, silver flame crackling in her hands, wings stretched beyond the bounds of the painting. She was someone to fear, or so this picture suggested.

Around the corner were more depictions of goddesses. Tallora continued forward, her heart elated at a portrait of Neoma and Staella upon a hill, hands clasped. *Pledge of Lovers,* the plaque read, and Tallora thought it wonderful.

She admired painting after painting—many showing brutality, one in particular of the battle between Neoma and Morathma, the world burning in silver flame behind them. A chill ran down her spine as she thought of the festival outside and the burning, smoldering snake.

Yet just as many displayed a side never spoken of outside Solvira—that there was humility to be found among their most powerful deity. One painting showed Neoma as a supplicant weeping before her wife, kneeling as the Goddess of Stars comforted her, and Tallora nearly cried for how dearly it touched her. Another showed her performing a sobering duty—she was the Goddess of the Moon, of Fertility and Creation, and here she comforted a new mother through childbirth, present in spirit as her translucent figure held the ailing woman. Tallora knew that even those not pledged to the Moon Goddess could pray for new life and for their baby's safe passage into the world. Neoma was not a goddess of love, but it was as she had said—she served her people. It was where true strength was found.

Tallora lingered at a depiction of Neoma and Ilune—the latter was a little girl, beaming bright as she giggled with life-like brilliance. Neoma held her, her joy unfettered as she kissed her daughter's cheek, and Tallora adored it so, this rare display of gentleness from the grandest deity of all.

Even the hardest of hearts craved softness sometimes.

Soon, Tallora returned to the closed door, where Dauriel spoke to her goddess. With her back against the opposite wall, she slid down, settling onto the floor.

This could be her kingdom.

Tallora thought of her forgotten vestments back at home beneath the sea and wondered if she could abandon them entirely to live a life in Solvira. A bittersweet joy swelled in her chest, but it brought far more questions than answers. Her exhausted mind could hardly contemplate it, still invigorated by the colorful atmosphere of the festival and of the presence in the room before her.

Yet she dwelled upon her beaded necklace of sea stars and pearls and the promises it held. Tallora shut her eyes and whispered aloud: *"Goddess Staella . . ."*

So strange, to feel immediate warmth in this cold hallway. A presence settled beside her, like the fireplaces in the castle libraries. Tallora smiled, swallowing a sudden rise of tears. Oh, she had missed this. She had not lost her faith, but she had abandoned any pursuit of it.

"I'm sorry for leaving you," she continued, her voice barely a whisper. "I hope you can accept a humble plea for forgiveness."

There were no words, no weight or movement, but Tallora felt a quiet, emphatic peace wash over her.

She smiled, her arms wrapping around herself. "I have a choice ahead. I know it's mine alone but..." She shut her eyes, contemplating her next phrase. The Triage believed in freewill above all, or so Neoma had said not minutes ago. "... keep my eyes open. Let me see all the signs so I may choose for myself and feel no regret."

She swore a spot of warmth touched her brow, as comforting as a mother's kiss. Then, the presence vanished, and Tallora was left in darkness.

The door creaked open then, loud amidst the silent hallway. Dauriel emerged, and Tallora caught a glimpse of a dormant statue behind her before the door slammed shut. Exhaustion fell upon her empress' features as she offered Tallora a hand to stand. "Neoma has spoken," Dauriel said softly, oddly monotone. "It is for my council and I to decide how to move forward."

Tallora kept a hold on her hand as she stepped lightly through the hallway. "I won't ask; I know I'm not allowed. But will you tell me if you need... anything?"

Dauriel's footsteps slowed and stopped, her features barely visible in the faint light. "Tonight, I simply need you," she replied, and Tallora kissed her in the darkness, her touch a precious thing.

They returned to the castle after, for the hour was late and Tallora's energy faltered. When they reached Dauriel's bedroom, the princess clung to her, vulnerability in her humble pose. Tallora kissed her hair and whispered, "We should sleep. You need rest."

Dauriel remained still, and Tallora wondered if she had heard, until she finally faced her, eyes glistening with tears. "Sorry. Sleep means tomorrow comes. Tomorrow means you leave."

"But not forever," Tallora assured, cupping Dauriel's cheek with her hand. "I promise. You'll see me again."

Tallora kissed her, helped her to remove her clothes, and coaxed her into bed, still nude, before removing her own. They slept in innocence, content to merely savor the other's presence.

There were reasons to fear the future, but Tallora forgot all of them in the gentle rhythm of Dauriel's breathing.

Chapter X 🐚

Tallora awoke at dawn, the sunrise casting soft beams of light through the open window. Beside her were Dauriel's gentle, lulling breaths, and Tallora settled against her naked chest, content to savor her skin.

Yet, to press their skin together only highlighted the thin sheen of sweat covering Tallora—apparently sleep had made a mess of her. She lingered a moment to breathe in Dauriel's scent, deeming the moment precious as time slipped further away.

Dauriel's offer remained. By Staella's Grace—it had nearly been a marriage proposal.

There were little details that made her shy. She remembered Dauriel's conviction to own the world, and she wouldn't lie and say she loved that. She thought of her mother, left alone in Stelune, and hoped she would understand. She thought of Kal and knew he would.

But she would be the Empress Consort of Solvira. She could surely visit her mother and loved ones at the places in between—at the beach, in the lake, even aboard a ship. Mother could visit and spend a few days in a tank if she could stomach it.

And perhaps she could whisper in her tyrannical wife's ear and temper her. She could spend her life with Dauriel. Oh, how her heart soared to consider it.

Though it pained her, she extracted herself from Dauriel's sleepy embrace, admiring the array of trinkets arranged on the walls and desk. Precious emblems, tiny crowns, flowers made from glass—beautiful things for their mistress to adore. Dauriel loved her dainty treasures, cherished them and treated them like gold. Warmth filled Tallora's heart as she looked back to her sleeping empress, vulnerable in the early hour. Morning light, filtered through the curtains, gently illuminated her face, the rest of her covered by her richly embroidered duvet.

The washroom held its own wonders—small statues, colorful soaps, a mirror gilded in gold. Tallora opened the curtain, letting light inside. In six months, she hadn't forgotten how to use a tub, and within minutes, she settled into a luxurious bath. The water smelled of jasmine, for old times' sake. Comforting, familiar warmth enveloped her.

She'd be casting aside the ocean for Dauriel, as she had put it. Tallora felt her heart sink at the thought, for she'd miss the beauty of her home. Her dream of becoming a priestess would be moot, thrown away for a far higher crown.

Yet, home held no beauty, these past six months without Dauriel.

Tallora rubbed soap along her arms and neck, loving the smell and the bubbles. Recalling how lovely she looked with her hair washed in mortal soaps, dried and curled, she dunked her head, prepared to surprise Dauriel with a vision of soft waves—

And then felt pain in her legs. Beneath the water, she gasped—by Staella's Grace, she could *gasp*—and though the pain settled quickly, she recognized the sensation sealing her legs together. Tallora's head burst from the water, but the damage had been done.

In the tub, Tallora stared in horror at her scaled, pink tail. The cry escaping her lips was pure shock, and when she lifted the sleek appendage, it splashed a small torrent of water across the bathroom.

Footsteps sounded beyond. Tallora shrunk as Dauriel burst in. "Tallora, what's wrong?"

"I—" Tallora stared at the water, at her tail beneath it, and the fine membranes of her fins draped over the edges of the tub, as crippling waves of embarrassment stilled her tongue. Oh, what would Dauriel think of her now? She loved her tail, all its power and might, but Dauriel loved human cunts, and

Tallora's hid beneath a sheath. Tears welled in her eyes.

All her memories of her mermaid body and Dauriel were met with shame.

Dauriel approached, naked and glorious, but no matter how tight Tallora curled in her bath, she couldn't hide her tail. The empress' eyes widened. "How?"

"I don't know," Tallora said softly, but then she remembered Harbinger's hurried words: '...*submerged in water*—' "I think the bath triggered it. I-I'm sorry."

"Don't be," Dauriel said, a hint of a smile on her lip. Her obliques shifted with every step forward. The jagged scars beneath her tattoos flexed with her forearm as she gripped the sides of the tub. "You didn't know—" Her words cut off, perhaps because of Tallora's tears. "Tallora—"

"Dauriel, you don't—" Tallora stopped when Dauriel stepped into the tub, her feet landing on either side of her tail.

Dauriel's hand gently skimmed the fuchsia scales as she settled beside her. "Gods, you're gorgeous."

The words brought boundless relief. She sniffed and wiped away her tears. "I think somewhere in my head, I'm still a beast to you."

"I always thought you were beautiful," Dauriel said, her lips placing soft kisses along Tallora's face. "Please, don't be embarrassed. We'll still be able to get you back to the lake. We just won't be able to ride together." She smiled; Tallora matched it, but still her stomach churned.

"Being beautiful and being a beast aren't mutually exclusive."

"I love *you*, Tallora." Her eyes spelled earnest sincerity, her hand gently stroking along Tallora's scales. "As a mermaid, as a human woman—even a De'Sindai, or whatever they turn you into next." Tallora's agitated nerves settled at Dauriel's kind chuckle. "You're not a beast. You're my beautiful Tallora, whose tail feels splendid to touch." Her hand suddenly faltered. "Am I allowed to touch it?"

Tallora laughed, and this time it was sincere. "It would be like touching someone's thigh."

"The scales aren't hard at all. Almost . . . amiable, like a leaf."

"A leaf!" Tallora laughed uproariously as she smacked Dauriel's hand. "It's good you're a Celestial; you'd be utterly uncharming as a mermaid."

"You wound me, fair maiden." Dauriel placed a hand on Tallora's cheek, her gentle touch juxtaposed wildly with her cruel smirk. "Then educate me—how would I charm and seduce a mermaid girl? Might be a different cunt, but I can still do wonders for your breasts."

Tallora grabbed Dauriel's hand, steadily leading it to land at her waist. "You might be the most arrogant ass I've ever met," she said, though her smile beamed like the sun. "Touch me. Kiss me. Do all you would for your favorite whores." Her wink, she prayed, was salacious. Dauriel's blush suggested she'd succeeded. "You'll know when it's time for more."

When Dauriel's hands skimmed her waist, Tallora's body, back to its true form, jolted in excitement, adoring those hands upon her. Her tail wrapped around Dauriel's leg, securing her there, as she might for a lover beneath the sea. She gasped when her empress massaged her breasts. "Speak up if I hurt you," Dauriel whispered in her ear.

"You won't." Tallora kissed the side of her mouth, back arching beneath Dauriel's touch, only for her breasts to be stolen by the empress' mouth.

Dauriel lavished praise upon her, her mouth and hands the pinnacle of worship. Tallora could do little to return the favor save for brush aside errant locks of her love's hair, but Dauriel, it seemed, had only Tallora's pleasure as her focus. With her legs straddling her body, Dauriel kissed her neck and breasts, one hand always at the juncture of her stomach and scales, her thumb brushing lines across them. "Enjoying my scales?" Tallora asked, and Dauriel's grin made her shiver.

"New is exciting," she replied simply, and Tallora thought she'd never felt more cherished.

In time, her gasping stole her wry comments, her body involuntarily relaxing, and Tallora grabbed Dauriel's hand. "Touch it slowly," she said, Dauriel's pupils a black hole in space. "I'm more sensitive than a human."

She led Dauriel's hand to her scales, to the small sheath prepared to part at the touch. It did so, like an anemone, and Dauriel, to her credit, did not flinch. She simply gazed down, removing their blessed eye contact, and lightly touched the parted edges, the flesh beneath it more sensitive than nerve. "You have no vulva."

"I don't need extra protection," Tallora replied, breathless beneath Dauriel's study and touch.

"Or a—"

"I do." Tallora grinned, her body aching at the teasing strokes. "My clit is inside. Right inside the top. You'll feel it."

"It's also much larger than I anticipated," Dauriel said, a boorish grin twisting her lip as she dipped her face down into the water—

And *licked* the parted edges.

The jolt of pleasure burst through Tallora's veins, nearly painful, as Dauriel's tongue skimmed along the edge of her parted lips and then her clit. Frantic breaths left her aching body.

Dauriel finally surfaced, triumphant and smug. "And you say they don't use their mouths beneath the sea?"

"Well, there's a risk," Tallora said, and that was as intelligent as she could phrase it.

"A risk?" Dauriel replied, drawing back her hand. She stared at her fingers, visibly contemplating between 'three' and 'four.'

Blood pulsed rapidly through Tallora's veins, her head spinning. She stole Dauriel's hand, shaking from absolute want. "Your whole hand, you darling idiot."

Dauriel closed her fist, an amused smirk at her lip. "Nothing I haven't done before." She lowered it down, and, *oh*, Tallora craved it so, but again reached down to stop her.

"It's going to latch onto . . ." Tallora suppressed a giggle at Dauriel's bafflement. "Men can't thrust well beneath the ocean without extra help. The water makes it difficult. My body will latch onto whatever you put in there, and it won't come out until I finish. That's why we don't use our tongues."

Dauriel nodded, noticeably intrigued. "It just means I would have to be careful."

This time, when Dauriel lowered her fist, Tallora quivered as her hand slipped inside, the friction delightful. She heard Dauriel's light gasp as Tallora's body tightened around it. "Now, you thrust," she managed, and for once, Dauriel simply obeyed.

"Fascinating," she heard Dauriel mutter.

To which she said, "Oh, shut up."

Dauriel did. Instead, she pleasured Tallora within and without, touching her breasts and romancing her with merely her stare. Tallora gasped at the divinity inside her, the absolute pleasure of Dauriel's touch, every thrust bringing her closer to completion.

And somewhere, down in the quiet recesses of her sound mind, Tallora felt an unspoken fear fade away—because Dauriel loved every part of her. Even her tail.

"Oh, Dauri—*el!*" she cried, her body convulsing, water spilling from the sides of the tub. Dauriel's hand touched her face as she rode out her pleasure, and when she'd finished, Tallora clutched that same hand and caressed it, kissed it, until her body finally stilled. She relaxed, and Dauriel withdrew her fist.

They matched eyes; Dauriel's were unspeakably soft. "You are wonderful," the empress whispered, coming to kiss Tallora's lips. "Tallora..." Her smile faded, melancholy settling to steal her joy. "Let me hold you, please?"

Dauriel pulled Tallora to her bare chest, her fingers separating the strands of her snow-white locks. Tallora shut her eyes, savoring the feeling, knowing their time must soon end. "Dauriel," she whispered, the feeling of those callused hands all she could ever want, "I do need to ask..." Her smile came unbidden, along with a joyous fluttering in her stomach. "How long must I wait before you'll accept an answer to your proposal?"

Lips caressed her hair. "I want you to return with Kal. Return to your home a final time and decide. I want you to hug your mother and tell her you love her before you decide you wish to live in my embrace instead. I want you to be *sure*," Dauriel finished. "You can't take it back, if only because of your duty as my spouse and as Empress Consort of Solvira. It wouldn't necessarily be a renouncing of citizenship, but you would pledge loyalty to Solvira and the Triage above all—fortunately you're already pledged to Staella. You are her priestess now, yes?"

"No," Tallora admitted, ashamed to say it out loud. "I tried to spend time in the temple, but I could barely leave my house for the first few weeks without being mobbed by people asking for 'The Great Survivor.' I'm something of a celebrity now." Bitterness sneered her lip, but Dauriel watched without judgement, merely kissed her cheek. "And going up to see the stars still brought me to tears. Thinking of her made me think too much of you. And I know that's pathetic, and it isn't fair to her, but I've had to be selfish in order to stay sane."

"Admittedly, I've gone every night to pray," Dauriel, said her expression gentle, "usually at the altar in the castle, but on full moons I go to the Temple of Unity. I feel closer to Neoma than I ever have before. Thinking of the day I stood physically before her makes me think of you, and that's something I've chased ever since you left."

Tallora drew idle lines across Dauriel's skin. "I suppose it means you're a stronger person than I am."

Dauriel shook her head. "Not stronger. Merely different. I was never allowed the luxury of running from my problems or sweeping them under the rug. Perhaps I'm resilient, but there's a curse in that too."

When Dauriel brought a hand up to caress her face, Tallora stared at the marks on her wrist, the runes and scars both. Dauriel did not run. She stood her ground and fought her opponents to the death—and sometimes the person to destroy was herself.

"If I stay with you, would I be able to see my mother?" Tallora asked, voicing her one reservation.

"We'll set up an entire underwater suite for your mother to stay in, if you'd like. We can even host the wedding by a beach. Untraditional, but you're hardly a traditional spouse."

Somehow, despite the offer of being an empress at Dauriel's side, the idea of having a wedding hadn't actually occurred to her until that blessed moment. She twisted in Dauriel's arms, their chests settling together as she suppressed a grin. "Wedding?"

"Wedding, yes. We'd have to have a wedding—"

Dauriel was interrupted by a noise Tallora couldn't quite name—only that it manifested from the depths of her soul and echoed as a *squeal.* "I hadn't even considered that! A *wedding!*" Again, she made that repugnantly delightful noise, squeezing Dauriel in her arms as she did.

Bafflement twisted Dauriel's lip. "That is what happens when royals marry," she said, a teasing glint in her eye. "I'm afraid if you want to be my wife, you'll have to suffer through a wedding—"

Again, Tallora squealed, and she couldn't have stopped it if she'd tried. She could hardly speak; she became a mass of giggles against Dauriel's chest.

"This isn't a proposal," Dauriel said, though not unkindly. "But it is something to keep in mind—"

Tallora shut her up with a kiss.

Dauriel wrapped Tallora in a cocoon of wet towels, giving no mind to the water soaking her doublet as she carried her out. Swaddled like an infant, Tallora leaned her head against her love's shoulder, the strength in her arms not lost on her, for Dauriel to carry both Tallora as her mermaid self and the wet towels.

They traversed the hallway with ease. "Answer this sincerely," Dauriel said. "Would you be uncomfortable spending time in a tank of water?"

Tallora shook her head. "With the promise of not being put on display again, you can do whatever you'd like."

"I do enjoy showing you off, I'll admit. But at my side. Not as a pet."

Gods, she was romantic. Tallora's cheeks flared. "Six months apart has turned you into a poet. Perhaps I should leave more often."

"Well, while you will be leaving, I hope it shall be weeks instead of months." They reached the lift; Tallora felt it travel up, watched the world shift beyond. "Do you want something to cover your body? Wandering eyes, and all."

Tallora shook her head. "It's still strange to me that you uplanders care. Unless this is just you being protective." She winked; Dauriel smiled.

"No, though I am remiss to share your breasts with anyone else."

"They're for your mouth only," Tallora replied, and despite their crass banter, Dauriel's visage bore unspeakable softness. Her lips pulled into a smile. "I'll be fine."

When they exited the lift, Tallora saw the great doors leading to the throne room ahead.

Standing beside it was Kal, his stance uncharacteristically tall. When he noticed them approach, his eyes widened. "Tallora, what happened?!"

"I took a bath. Being submerged in water dispels Harbinger's spell."

Kal visibly fought a grin, then seemed to notice Dauriel was the one carrying her. "Oh! Empress Dauriel." He bowed low. "Good morning. The rest of your council is inside—they asked me to tell you that."

She glanced to the doorknob. "Would you mind..?"

Kal was kind enough to twist the knob. Dauriel didn't enter farther than the doorway. "Adrael! Come here."

Tallora watched the magister leave his place among the small collection of people ahead, all standing before an empty throne. "Your majesty?" he said, once he neared.

"Tallora, as you might have noticed, is in need of water."

He didn't ask, but Tallora watched him raise his arms and perform a familiar spell. Condensation escaped from the towels, from the air, gathering in an ever-expanding sphere before them. When it had grown to accommodate her size, Dauriel let what towels she could fall away without risking Tallora dropping to the ground.

With care, she sank her arms and Tallora within the sphere, but before she could withdraw, Tallora stole her hand and kissed it.

Dauriel leaned forward, and at the barrier of air and water, their lips met. "I don't intend to let the meeting last too long."

"I'll manage, somehow," Tallora replied, her smile teasing.

Dauriel left, but not without a lingering glance, cut off only when the door shut.

"What's a bath?"

Tallora looked to Kal, who stared earnestly from beyond her large bubble. "It's water in a tub. They fill it to clean themselves."

"Why were you in a bath?"

"Because uplander bodies dirty quickly."

Kal looked down at his clothing, the same as the night before, inspecting himself. "Do I need a bath?"

"I can't smell you, so I wouldn't know. But likely not, unless you've been sweating."

His slight frown was enough to betray him.

Tallora laughed. "What in Tortalga's Sea did you do to get sweaty, Kal? Aside from running from guards."

Kal hesitated a moment too long.

Now, Tallora frowned. "Kal?"

"Likely the same thing you did."

Tallora studied his darling face as he bit his lip, his eyes refusing to meet hers as a blush filled his cheeks. "You . . ." She covered her mouth as his implications fell together. "With Leah!"

"Well, after you left, Leah and I—"

"You went to the festival!" Tallora stared, mouth agape. "We saw you but didn't want to bother you. You fucked my friend!"

"You fucked your empress. I don't think I did anything wrong."

Tallora laughed, a flood of unexpected joy washing over her. "Oh, Kal . . . You are inexplicable."

His shy smile spoke volumes. "She, Mocum, and I went to the festival and had a wonderful time, but once she took Mocum home to sleep, she, uh . . ."

His blush brightened. "Well, she started it. Honestly, I'm a little sad to leave."

"One fuck and you fall in love," Tallora teased, a slight 'tsk tsk' accompanying her words.

Kal's stare was as indignant as she'd ever seen from the boy. "It was more than once." Tallora simply laughed, ignoring his frown. "And I'm not in love. She is exceptionally charming, though. I . . . could be."

Tallora swallowed her giggles, instead settling on a smile. "Kal, Leah saved my life. More than once. She's as dear to me as anyone beneath the waves, and I can't think of a better man for her than you, in part because I can't think of a better man than you." Mischief filled her gaze, and before she could stop herself, she added, "So if you fucked her to spite me, I'm sorry but it didn't work."

"It was only a guppy's worth of my motivation." They shared a smile, an understanding in the gesture Tallora was relieved to see—they could remain friends.

A comfortable silence settled, but Tallora's mind expelled a final thought. "Kal, do tell me if this is inappropriate, but uplander sex is odd. Pleasant, but odd."

"Agreed," he replied, his blush returning. "It's messier. Leah was kind enough to explain it all. I think she thought it was funny that I didn't know."

Tallora giggled, the memory of her first time with Dauriel bringing its own blush.

"And to, uh, answer our question from yesterday . . ." Kal's blush blossomed deeper, red coloring nearly his entire face. "It does get bigger when aroused."

Her laughter increased, embarrassed at the thought. "Mystery solved."

The doorknob twisted then. Dauriel emerged, looking oddly somber. "Come with me," she said, straightening her stance. Adrael approached from behind; Dauriel gestured toward Tallora, then turned on her heels.

Kal followed, as did Tallora when her bubble moved at Adrael's behest. She focused on the world beyond, upon Dauriel's cape as it swayed with every powerful step she took.

Dauriel took her place on her throne, a spectacle as she gazed down upon the rest. All of her inner council was in attendance, with Priestess Greyva and her owl familiar perched on her arm, Priest Rel and that monstrous, bald bird, and the new Priestess Toria—who had no bird, but in her hands she held a small bat. "Prince Kalvin," Dauriel said, her tone bearing all the authority of her station, "my council and I have spoken, and we have agreed it is best if I speak to your father. You've made it clear that there are grievous misunderstandings between our two kingdoms, and whatever the outcome of all this, I don't want there to be any question of the truth."

Kal beamed. "Empress Dauriel, thank you."

"Your words have made it clear that there are misunderstandings not only between my kingdom and yours, but between us and Moratham—and, perhaps, between the two of you as well. And so I shall meet with Moratham immediately."

The words were shocking, yes—and it showed on both she and Kal's faces.

"I fear our pride as rulers has prevented us from having the civil discussion we need to move forward," Dauriel continued. "I would propose, with your support, something to clear the air. A summit—I shall meet in person with your father, just as I shall invite Moratham to discuss the disagreements between us."

"Empress Dauriel, this is wonderful," Kal said, daring to step forward. "I'm confident my father will agree."

"To soothe the inevitable awkward conversation between Moratham and myself, I would ask that you stay just a few more minutes."

Kal nodded, though it was clear by his earnest expression that he had no idea what Dauriel meant by that. Tallora didn't either, and she watched closely as Dauriel withdrew a tied scroll from a table beside her throne. She pulled the string but discarded the parchment, letting it fall to the floor. Instead, she held the small pouch attached to the string, opened it with care, and dumped what appeared to be a pile of sand into her palm.

She blew a gentle breath, then sat back, legs spread wide as the sand flew into the air. But it did not settle peacefully onto the floor; instead, it swirled as a small tornado, slowly gaining shape and substance. Tallora watched in amazement as the sand created a figure, and though only mostly formed, it was one she recognized.

Ambassador Amulon. He looked as baffled as she but quickly righted himself as the sand solidified. His movements betrayed the spell—every motion sent small bits of sand scattering about the throne room. But his voice spoke with perfect clarity. "Empress Dauriel—a delight and a surprise."

He bowed, and Dauriel smiled, though it was the sort to send a shiver down Tallora's spine. "Ambassador Amulon, I can't say the same—especially with the knowledge that you've been colluding with the Tortalgan Sea to start a war against my people."

Amulon visibly paled, but Tallora was confident she had paled as well. "Esteemed Empress, I—"

"...have been colluding with your allies behind my back for military support in preparation for our inevitable conflict. Look behind you."

He did, his eyes widening when they settled onto Tallora and Kal—his expression a mirror to Tallora's, whose stomach knotted at Dauriel's words.

"Forgive me, Empress Dauriel," Amulon said, and behind his back, Tallora watched his hands clench the other, "but it seems you know something I do not."

"These two have come and requested I speak to King Merl of the Tortalgan Sea and clear any misconceptions between us. But in speaking to them, it's become increasingly clear that you and I don't understand the other either. I would propose something different."

Amulon nodded, and though Tallora couldn't see his face, she could imagine the forced neutrality nonetheless. "Do tell."

"Peace, Amulon."

The words lingered in the air, easing the tension by slow degrees. Dauriel stood from her throne and leisurely descended the steps. "Prince Kalvin has informed me of the appalling pieces of misinformation circulating through our trio of kingdoms—misinformation regarding Tallora, regarding you and your Speaker, regarding me—and has proposed a plan to set all records straight: a summit. Solvira would gladly host it. A summit wherein the Speaker and King Merl could come and listen and of course be given the chance to speak their grievances. The disagreements between our kingdoms continue, but truthfully, war between us all would lead to a death toll none of us can truly fathom—why provoke conflict when this might be resolved with a simple conversation?"

Amulon stared as though she'd spoken Demoni, but he didn't look displeased. "This will require a conversation with the Speaker—"

"Of course," Dauriel said, near enough to decapitate him, had she wielded a sword. She stood with as much gallantry to accomplish it.

". . . but I believe he will see the merit of this plan."

Tallora saw Kal's grin and couldn't help but match it.

"There is much more to discuss," Dauriel said, "but first we need his agreement. Tell him I would happily meet with him and speak as rulers to resolve the dispute at the border—perhaps I've been misguided. I think we can come to a compromise."

148

The words sat unwell with Tallora, but Amulon's enthused nod conveyed only approval. "I will deliver the news straightaway."

"You may be dismissed. We shall be in contact soon to discuss the details. I shall escort our merfolk guests back to the lake so they might deliver the news as well."

Amulon bowed to Dauriel, then offered an approving nod to Kal, his smile genuine, as far as Tallora could see. The sand dissolved, falling as merely a pile upon the glass floor.

Dauriel approached Kal. "We would like to meet with your father, Kalvin." From her pocket, she procured a small mirror—which Tallora realized she had seen before, when Dauriel had communicated with Empress Vahla a lifetime ago. "Face to face, but if you tap the mirror's reflection, we can communicate in the meantime."

Kal accepted the offering, slipping it quickly into his pocket. "Thank you, Empress Dauriel."

"While I can't speak with any precision," Dauriel replied, looking to Tallora now, "I believe your time grows short. We should bring the two of you to the lake."

Tallora nodded, her heart aching at the thought.

Soon, Kal sat in a carriage with General Khastra and Magister Adrael, a volley of guards on horseback around them. Dauriel rode on her own steed, and Tallora thought of Tycus, the horse the empress had once loved.

This one was sleek and lithe, like she herself, their colors matching as Dauriel rode in an ensemble of black, her adornments of silver subtle and rich. Tallora floated in her bubble beside them, tethered to nothing it seemed, yet she moved along unbidden, remaining near enough to Dauriel to speak. "Do you truly mean to compromise about the border dispute?"

Dauriel looked to her with scrutiny, though it quickly fell into a glower. "No. I am willing to reopen the discussion though—there are few wounds money can't fix, and it would be a weakness for me to have to pay to have my citizens back."

"Perhaps if you offer back the money they gave your mother, they'd consider it fair."

Dauriel's expression softened. "As always, your wisdom is invaluable. I see the merit."

Tallora blushed bright, Dauriel's adoring gaze certain to warm her for days to come. "Assuming Harbinger kept her word," she said, grinning at the people watching—she was an odd sight as she floated in her bubble, with her tail and pearlescent skin, "we should be returning to Stelune before the end of the day. She can travel through Sha'Demoni."

"Fascinating. It's a rare gift, even among De'Sindai with potent demon blood. Khastra can't do it."

Emblems of the previous night's festival remained as they rode through the streets—stalls not yet disassembled, evidence of soot on the ground. The platform remained, the ashes of the wooden snake an omen of Solvira's bloody history. "My point," she said, looking back to Dauriel's familiar face, "is things might move quickly. I'd like to tell my mother about you."

"Of course." Dauriel's grin outshone the blissful sun.

"My mother is wonderful. And I think she'd like you, if only because I do. I still worry how she'd fare without me, though."

"Well, as the mother to the empress consort, she would be supported by the treasury. If you're worried for her business, she won't have to work if she doesn't want to." Dauriel's expression held no grandiose or mischief, simply pure practicality. Tallora smiled, her heart threatening to burst.

"Truthfully, Tallora," Dauriel continued, solemn as she removed her gaze, "even if you deny me, I would grant you and your family the protection of the crown all your life. Whatever you could ever want or need, I would give you. My love isn't conditional upon you giving up your home for me."

A pit expanded in Tallora's stomach, to hear those words. Try as she might, she couldn't breach the barrier and touch Dauriel's hand. "You know I won't deny you."

"I don't know that," Dauriel replied soberly, but the devotion in her gaze remained constant. "The pressures and dangers of ruling Solvira aren't the sort I'd wish upon anyone, and I was prepared for it from birth. My life is hardly charmed. I worry you don't know what you're agreeing to."

An objection sat on her tongue, a longing to reject Dauriel's notion, but fondness remained in those silver eyes, and Tallora realized this had nothing to do with love. Instead . . .

Her words conveyed reality, that Tallora's life would change forever in ways she could not foresee. She had a choice.

Though her heart still settled in Solvira, she nodded. "I promise, when I give you my answer, I'll be sure. Perhaps at the summit, assuming all goes according to plan."

Dauriel's smile faded. "It would be best if you weren't at the summit. Not because of anything you've done, but you could so easily be wielded as a weapon against Solvira. Imagine the Speaker holds a knife to your throat as he hands me a treaty—or even your own king, assuming he knows your worth to me."

"Kal would never let that happen—"

"Whatever his influence, he doesn't rule the seas." Dauriel's subtle frown pled, and Tallora's heart ached to see it. "Be safe, above all."

They passed the city gates, lapsing into silence as their party left the road and shifted their path toward the massive lake. With care to keep the reins tight, Dauriel swiftly removed her glove and brought her hand to Tallora's bubble, easily sinking it inside.

Tallora grasped it. They held hands as they approached their farewell.

When the carriage stopped beside the lake, Kal quickly emerged, followed by Adrael. Tallora waited for Khastra, but the general seemed content to remain inside.

"Mer—*Tallora.*" Tallora turned to the magister. "Are you ready?"

Tallora looked to the lake, how it glistened, the border hardly visible from the shore. "I suppose—"

"Let me hold her." Tallora looked to Dauriel, who gazed at her in earnest as she dismounted her horse. "If she'll allow it."

Tallora nodded slowly, no longer worried for Kal's feelings. Dauriel held her arms out as she approached, the bubble lowering to match—

It burst, splattering their party with water. But Dauriel simply laughed as Tallora fell those last few inches, uncaring of the water soaking her doublet. Smoothly, mockingly so, she said, "Tallora, may I just say that your tail beneath the sunlight is the loveliest sight I've ever seen."

"You may *not,* you flattering fool," she replied, her arms looped around Dauriel's neck. With her lips to her ear, she gave a slight nip to her lobe. "Not in public, anyway."

They kissed, and Tallora forgot the world—

Until it bombarded into her space, when Khastra suddenly burst from the carriage. *"Yoon!"*

Tallora pulled back, immediately following her stare, and saw Harbinger swimming just beyond the shore. The Onian's eye bore the reflection of an onyx disk, perfectly round as she looked back to Khastra and said, "Damn it."

"Daughter of Yu'Khrall, Granddaughter of Onias," Khastra said, her grin vicious, revealing her teeth. "I thought this might be your mischief."

Kal was kind enough to voice everyone's question. "You know each other?"

"We do not," Harbinger replied, tentacles visible as she swam closer to shore, "but we do know *of* each other. Hello, Daughter of Ku'Shya—"

"Wait!" Tallora stared at Harbinger, the reality of Khastra's words suddenly falling together. "Did you say *Onias?*"

"She did."

"You're the *granddaughter* of Onias? The demon god?"

"That is also correct."

And . . . *Yu'Khrall.* The monster in the mural.

Tallora looked to Khastra, the weight of the title *Daughter of Ku'Shya* also not lost on her. Fitting that the Demon Goddess of War would birth the Bringer of War.

Visibly triumphant, Khastra stared down the granddaughter of her rival god. The half-demon chuckled. "'Harbinger' is hardly a subtle name." She glanced to the rest of them, amusement etched onto her elegant face. "Her name is 'Yoon.' In Demoni, Yoon loosely translates into the Solviran word 'harbinger.'" She looked back to Harbinger—Yoon. "Are you even trying to hide?"

Harbinger's unnerving gaze fixed upon Khastra like a black hole. "You are the first one who has guessed it."

"Yu'Khrall!" Tallora exclaimed, the truth expanding like air in her chest. "That's how you know—?!" Tallora struggled to articulate her words, all the world suddenly falling into place.

Harbinger smiled wide, revealing her teeth. But Khastra did not—quite the opposite, with how fiercely she glowered. "I beg your pardon?"

Kal looked equally baffled. "Tallora, what are you talking about?"

Tallora clung to Dauriel, watching realization settle onto her face as well, then said, "Dauriel knew the mural—the one from the cave." She quickly explained all that Dauriel had said regarding Yu'Khrall and Neoma, the story and the key to his prison. "I don't know if it soothes my fears or not," she finished, noting Kal's thoughtful expression, "but this must be what they were trying to do." The pit in her stomach only expanded at the words. She looked to Harbinger, noting the glee in her eye.

Khastra openly glowered. "You are cheerful at the thought of Yu'Khrall's return."

"She's cursed to say nothing about it," Tallora explained, and Harbinger held up her arm, revealing the brand. "I think she's happy someone else said it."

Khastra approached the shore, beckoning for Harbinger to meet her. Though visibly hesitant, Harbinger obeyed, remaining in the water as the half-demon knelt beside her. When she offered her arm, Khastra's glowing eyes narrowed. "We could cut it off."

Tallora flinched at the suggestion, but to her horror, Harbinger seemed to consider it. "Hold on!" Tallora cried, and in Dauriel's embrace, she shook her head. "Cutting off limbs seems a little excessive."

"She has extra."

Harbinger lifted a single tentacle above the water and waved it. "It will hurt, but it will grow back eventually."

"Yes, but rather than resorting this quickly to dismemberment—" Tallora grimaced at the mere idea, her own arms hurting in solidarity. "Harbinger, is there anything more we *need* to know?"

Harbinger stared, her expression difficult to decipher given she had one eye and no eyebrow. "Perhaps, but . . ." She cringed as she asked, "You are doing peace talks?"

"We are, indeed," Dauriel replied. Despite the circumstances, Tallora savored the few extra minutes of touch.

"Then, it should be fine."

Khastra stood back up, towering over the rest of them by far. "I can speak with Goddess Ilune. Would that soothe your fears?"

"I fear Goddess Ilune's sentiments," Harbinger said, still noticeably stiff, "but I trust that you understand the seriousness of the situation more than anyone, Bringer of War. If you believe she would be of help, I shall say yes. Perhaps she can say what I cannot."

"Perhaps she will say whatever Neoma would not," Dauriel said softly, for only Tallora to hear. "She did not deny that Yu'Khrall is a threat, but did remind me that the power to free him truly is only delegated to only one."

Tallora wouldn't say she felt relief, but some weight had lifted. "Then all will be well."

"My question," Khastra muttered, "is why would they be so stupid? Do they think they can control him?"

Harbinger heaved a loud and dramatic sigh, her glower cast to her brutalized arm. "Perhaps Goddess Ilune will know that as well."

Tallora spared a glance for Kal, who stared at the water's edge, perhaps contemplating their guide's words. She looked back to Dauriel, smoothly meeting her lips. "You'll hear from me soon," she said, finality in the phrase. Her fingers stroked Dauriel's dark locks, adoring the short hair, loving every piece of this woman. Her heart ached, but she held hope of seeing her again, and soon. "I love you."

"I love you too, Tallora."

They kissed. They lingered. Only when a tentative cough interrupted them did they part. Harbinger waved from within the water. "Your prince will be transforming any moment now. You have to say goodbye."

As Kal stripped himself of clothing, Dauriel slowly approached the shore, kneeling before the water's edge. "No matter what the future brings, my love for you is as constant as the rising moon."

"You're sounding awfully ominous," Tallora teased, though the words unsettled her, an odd apprehension filling her gut.

"Silly me," Dauriel replied, and with a final kiss, she helped Tallora return to the lake. Cool water enveloped her. She clung to Dauriel's arm as Kal joined her, disappearing beneath the waves, his transformation surely happening beside them.

But she and Dauriel simply touched, the moment binding and assured.

Soon enough, Kal emerged from the water, his mop of blue hair thoroughly drenched. Dauriel gently lifted Tallora's hand, bringing it to her lips. Her lingering kiss brought Tallora hope. "Be safe. And bear in mind that you're more than invited to steal that mirror from Kal. I shall send an entire armada to fetch you, if that's what it takes."

Tallora nodded as Dauriel released her. "You'll hear from me soon."

Dauriel stood. They did not say goodbye; Tallora blew a kiss and dove beneath the waves.

Chapter XI 🐚

They travelled largely in silence, each too lost in their own inner worlds. Kal occasionally voiced thoughts of Yu'Khrall but nothing of note, except—

"Harbinger, does this mean my father condoned what happened to you?"

Harbinger said nothing, but the exhaustion in her eye suggested his guess was true.

Despite the stakes before them, Tallora thought of Dauriel, her heart still filled to the brim with warmth. They would be married—as impossible and perfect a future as she could have ever wished for. Tallora missed her already, but their reunion was inevitable.

And so when they emerged from the shadows before the canyon housing Stelune, she still beamed from ear to ear.

Kal said, "Harbinger, if this goes well, you'll be a hero. I'll be certain you're rewarded for your service to the crown."

"You would reward me best by letting me return to my isolated life," Harbinger replied, her one eye fixed upon him. "Good luck."

Tallora offered a hand, gracious when Harbinger accepted it. "Thank you for everything."

"If you are truly grateful, you will give me your hair."

Harbinger grinned wide, those shark teeth forever daunting. Tallora grimaced as she plucked out a single strand and offered it forward. "Why though?"

"In case I need to find you again."

The Onian wrapped the strand around her finger and said her farewell to Kal. Tallora, however, stared off into the distant reefs, her fluttering heart still warm, yet in the moment of silence, a strange hesitation filled her, to gaze upon the wonders of her beloved home.

"Tallora?"

When Tallora looked to Kal, Harbinger had already disappeared.

"Will you come with me to the castle?"

Tallora nodded, joining Kal as he swam toward the city.

The city lights shone even in the day, its beauty striking Tallora in ways it never had before. The colorful coral at the outskirts held a vibrancy to rival upper-world flowers, and Tallora loved it so, unable to deny the splendor of her home. The city beneath the sea flourished, and she wondered how she would take its loss.

What would be worse—to lose her home or lose her heart?

As they swam down into the canals, people parted for the prince in their midst. They passed near enough Tallora's shop for her heart to yearn. She missed her mother, but the time would soon come to tell her news of joy, that she'd just reunited with the love of her life.

She followed Kal to the castle. The guards looked aghast at their approach. "Your Highness! Your father has been searching for you."

"I have an explanation, and I hope he'll understand. Will you inform him that I've returned?"

One guard nodded and swam inside. Kal gestured for Tallora to follow. He escorted her to the throne room, vacant for the moment, and whispered, "Let me talk. He'll be less inclined to be furious with me than with you."

Tallora nodded, and soon King Merl entered, with Queen Fauln following behind. She immediately swam to Kal and embraced him. "My son, where have you been?!"

Merl also approached, gripping Kal tight in his strong arms. But his stare fell to Tallora, his countenance settling into a glare. "I do hope you have a proper explanation for why you've gone and disappeared with this woman."

The blatant accusation boiled Tallora's blood, but Kal pulled away and said, "Father, it was my idea—not hers. I simply needed her support, and I think you'll understand why once I've said my piece."

Advisor Chemon peeked his head in, visibly confused to see them there. He swam to his spot beside the throne.

"The time is yours, Kal," Merl said, his lips a thin line.

"Father, the fact of the matter is I can't stand the thought of us entering a war on false pretenses," Kal began. Tallora watched his stance grow taller, every bit the monarch as he faced his father.

"False pretenses?"

"The conflict between Moratham and Solvira is based upon nothing but misinformation and petty, ancient feuds. For us to tie ourselves to it would be a death sentence. I couldn't stand idly by for that. And so, without the knowledge of the crown, I sought action. I returned to the witch, Harbinger, with the intention of sending a message to Solvira—which is why I asked Tallora to accompany me, since I knew they would listen if the words came from her—"

"You spoke to Solvira!" King Merl had turned red, every bit of him stiff.

"You said I could—"

"You should be locked in the dungeon for treason! Both of you!" he added, staring daggers at Tallora. *"Do you realize what you've done?!"*

Kal crossed his arms, calm in the face of his father's fury. "I have a plan to end this conflict once and for all—with *peace.* That is what you want, isn't it? Or has Moratham offered to buy our principles as well as our trust?"

Merl's glare could have melted a glacier, but he shut his mouth. "Continue," he seethed.

Kal resumed his account, telling of the journey to the witch—though without landmarks, thank the Stars—of their transformation, their trip. "The crown received us graciously," Kal said, though perhaps skimming a few details. "Empress Dauriel and her council heard us out and agreed we would all benefit from meeting. She would like to speak with you and has offered the opportunity for a summit."

Merl had glared at Tallora for most of the account, but at the word 'summit,' he turned to Kal and said, "A what?"

"A meeting between our respective rulers, to discuss this as civilized people and make amends. But rather than have me explain . . ." From his satchel, he withdrew the gifted mirror, pure silver and able to fit in only one hand. "Empress Dauriel would happily explain it herself."

Merl accepted the offered trinket, frowning as he stared at the silver sheen. "You're quick to side with Solvira instead of your own country."

"Solvira isn't the country set on releasing a leviathan into the seas," Kal replied, and even Tallora balked at the bitterness in the words. "That was your plan, wasn't it? To release the fabled Yu'Khrall?"

"A bold assumption."

"Then tell me it's a lie."

Kal's statement lingered like a noxious cloud, poisoning the air with each passing second. Sneering, Merl said, "Yu'Khrall despises Solvira. He'd be our greatest defense—"

"Even if that were true, what, by Tortalga's Grace, makes you think he'd listen? More than likely he'd destroy us on the path to Solvira!"

"You assume he's a beast, but he holds as much intelligence as you or I—he can be reasoned with—"

"Then why not call upon Yaleris, the dragon? Or perhaps we simply swim away from any further negotiations with Moratham and remove ourselves as any kind of threat—"

"Kalvin—!" King Merl bit back his cry, fury permanently etched into his aging features. "I am proud of your ambition," he said, stiff and muted. "I only wish you would do more listening than talking."

"I listened a great deal to Empress Dauriel this past day and night," Kal said, his own tone subdued and pleading, "and to paint her as a monster is a disservice to us both."

Merl returned his seething attention to the mirror, his frown slowly fading. "And what role did Tallora have in all of this?"

"Truthfully," Kal replied, an easy smile on his lips, "she convinced the Solviran Royals that I truly was a prince of the sea and not a raving lunatic."

"Her loyalties are compromised," Merl said, and Tallora felt sick at the words. He did not look at her, his stare only for Kal. "For all we know, she's manipulated you into selling our kingdom to Solvira—you've revealed our subterfuge, and now we risk ruin."

"How could Tallora have manipulated me when the whole affair was my plan?"

"She's softened you to the Solviran cause—"

"She's barely spoken of them—"

"Kalvin, can you honestly say there is nothing strange about her behavior?"

Kal looked to Tallora, his large eyes offering the smile his stoic face could not. "Father, I trust Tallora. But more importantly, I trust that Solvira trusts her. Let her speak for herself."

King Merl cast his scrutinizing glare to her. "Convince me, Tallora. Tell me that Solvira holds no subterfuge or threat."

Tallora swam forward, steeling her courage as she said, "Your majesty, I don't know what you want me to say. If you wish for me to speak on behalf of Empress Dauriel's character, I swear to you she's a woman of honor. She's lived a difficult life—despite her royal upbringing, she was treated as a pariah by her own family after a sickness nearly took her life. And though she stole me from the ocean, she's done all in her power to rectify that wrong—including ruin her reputation to save my life, more than once. Staella forgave her, and so have I. Solvira holds the most powerful army in the world, and so of course they're a threat. But armies march at their leader's command. Whatever her stances and her beliefs, I swear to you, King Merl—if she's given her word, there is no force on earth that would cause her to falter. If she says she wishes to meet and discuss peace, she intends to do nothing less."

The tension had steadily faded with Tallora's words, leaving only thoughtful faces, including King Merl's.

Kal spoke first. "You said you would at least speak to her."

Merl looked to the mirror. "Leave us. All of you. I would speak to Empress Dauriel alone, as King of the Tortalgan Sea."

Tallora could not say if she felt relieved, but when Kal beckoned for her to follow, a sense of finality settled. She had done all she could.

The backstreets of the city were a less travelled path, so the journey home passed quickly. After a hasty farewell to Kal, Tallora swam up to the floor that was hers, and even before she'd had the chance to touch the door, her mother rolled it aside. "Momma, I—"

Her mother's tears reminded her of six months prior, when Tallora had returned from Solvira. Here she floated once more, her mother's arms around her. "Oh, my Tallora," her mother wept, heaving great sobs into her shoulder.

"I'm safe," she said, stroking Mother's graying-strands of hair. "Let's go inside. I have so much to tell you."

She escorted her mother into their modest home, wondering if, with the promise of Solvira's wealth, her mother might choose something nicer. Her mother certainly deserved it, having worked for years in their shop with little reward. They lived a humble life—what would it mean, to suddenly be gifted riches unbound?

When she'd helped her mother sit in one of the curved chairs, Tallora floated before her. "I went to Solvira."

Panic etched itself onto her mother's face. "What?!"

"Listen. Kal and I were on a mission to stop a war, and I'm so sorry I didn't tell you. But I couldn't let your life be in danger."

Her mother spared a glance to the window, the bars preventing entry. "Castle guards came here, looking for Prince Kalvin. I told them the truth—that I knew nothing, but they were right in thinking he was off gallivanting with you."

They shared a smile, though Mother's eyes still held tears. "It's a long story, but Kal and I found an Onian Witch who helped us travel quickly and gave us uplander legs so we could speak to Solvira's Council. Our quest has been successful so far—the empress has agreed to meet with King Merl and the Speaker. There are so many rumors floating around. Kal wants to stop needless bloodshed, and I think we might have."

Tallora's mother smiled, eyes wide and watery but genuine happiness flickered on her features. "You terrify me, my little hero. Is this the end of it, then?"

"I don't know," Tallora said truthfully, hating how her mother's expression fell. "There is going to be a summit, and the outcome will determine the future of our kingdom's peace. I pray my part is done. But aside from politics . . ." As she gathered her thoughts, Tallora fought a smile, knowing her words would be bittersweet. "Momma, there's someone I love."

"You told me of Leah."

"I adore Leah, but I lied. She was never more than a friend to me. There's someone else, but I couldn't say who. The secret was too dangerous, even if all of Solvira suspects it. But I couldn't confirm it. I couldn't tell you, even though my heart was breaking every day to stay silent. Momma..." She released a breath, bracing for a reaction she could not predict. "I'm in love with Empress Dauriel Solviraes. And she loves me too, with all her heart."

Her mother stared, her slack-jaw a mystery Tallora couldn't decipher. "The *empress?*"

"Yes."

Each second her mother said nothing, Tallora felt her blood grow colder. "I—" Her mother's words cut off. She looked to the window, unable to meet Tallora's eye. "I don't know what to say to that."

"She's nothing like you've heard," Tallora pled, yet her voice could hardly breach above a whisper. "Momma, she's good. I've never loved anyone the way I love her. When I went to see her, it was as though I'd never left. She loves me, I swear it. Goddess Staella spared her life because of it."

Again, her mother was silent, her hand reaching up to clasp her own bony shoulder. Tallora wondered when she'd grown so frail. "You did say Goddess Staella pardoned her."

"She pardoned her because of my forgiveness and because Dauriel's heart had changed. Momma, when I met her, she was bitter and broken. I didn't mean to help her. I hated her, yet we grew to be friends. And then we were something more."

"So the rumors of her raping you—"

"Aren't true at all!" Tallora bit back her sudden spike in emotion, the words too wicked to even speak. "No. She treats me like gold. She and I..." She swallowed the rising lump in her throat, knowing the words must be said, even if they hurt. "She wants to marry me." When Momma simply stared, she added, "I would be Empress Consort Tallora Solviraes."

"I know," her mother said, yet her words had become stone.

"A-And it wouldn't mean I'd never see you again. I could visit. You could visit. Dauriel has offered a stipend from the treasury for you, as my mother. You'd have a place to stay in the palace and all the money you could need down here—"

"Tallora, do you hear yourself?"

The words, so soft, managed to shatter Tallora's perfect world. "What?"

"My darling," her momma pled, her tears having never staunched, gently glistening before they disappeared into the water, "I don't think you understand what Solvira is. The Solviraes are tyrants. They're warmongers. They're *evil*, and the whole world should fear them."

Aghast, Tallora struggled to find her voice. "B-But they're Neoma's lineage—"

"Bless Staella, but her daughter is wicked, and her lineage takes after her. Tallora, I don't doubt you love her, but do you love her more than your people? Your heritage? You wouldn't simply be leaving us; you'd be betraying us."

Tears welled in Tallora's eyes, the earnest words shattering her hope. "Dauriel is different."

But the words were a lie. She recalled Dauriel's speech upon the balcony, of her dream to destroy Moratham. She remembered long ago, her dream of slaying a dragon, to have a legacy the world might fear. Dauriel had grown, had learned to love and be loved, but she was still herself: ambitious and dangerous.

"I'm not trying to hurt you," her mother said, still curled up in her seat, gazing up at Tallora in a supplicant's stance. "I love you with all my heart, but I can't condone this. If she were anyone else in Solvira, I'd be overjoyed. It's not the citizens who make life hell for the rest of the world—it's those at the top. Perhaps her love for you is genuine—"

"It is," Tallora said, fighting to keep composed.

"All right—her love is genuine. But who she is to you and who she is to the world are very different."

Dauriel alone held vulnerabilities Tallora helped her overcome, gently coaxing her to reveal every part of herself. But to others she was brash and cold.

Yet Tallora still wanted her. By Staella's Grace, she wanted her with all her heart. "She didn't want me to accept the offer immediately," Tallora whispered, hoping to salvage her beloved's character. "She wanted me to be certain I was sure. Even if I don't accept, she's offered us Solvira's protection and funding because she cares. She simply wants me safe and comfortable."

"That's altruistic of her," Momma said, releasing a weighted sigh. Her hands clasped the other, turning white. "And while you are welcome to accept, I will politely decline. I cannot accept Solviran aid. Not when tensions are so explosive."

"That's why Kal and I went. To try and ease those tensions. We want peace. She wants peace. She's ambitious, yes, but she isn't bloodthirsty. We've planned a summit for *peace.*"

In slow measures, like swimming through ink, Momma came to envelop Tallora in a hug. "My Tallora, know that I will love you no matter what you choose. But I won't approve. I can't."

"Would you come to the wedding?" Tallora asked, voice threatening to break.

"I would have to think on it." When she pulled back, her smile held sorrow. She blinked, and the sea carried away her tears. "Tell me about your trip. You'll have to explain how you and Kal came and went in only days."

"Later. I . . ." Tallora shut her eyes, her tears finally escaping. Outside, the world turned, the noise of the city bustling, yet her own world lay uncertain, and she desperately wished for it to slow. "I need to be alone."

166

Her momma watched, regret in her familiar, lovely features as Tallora swam to her room, curled upon her bed, and softly cried.

Royalty called to her, but not for its title, though it would come whether she liked it or not. Her mother had spoken no lies. But Tallora's heart yearned, all the same.

Sleep soon stole her. When she opened her eyes, the world had darkened, and a gentle voice said, "Tallora?"

Tallora rubbed exhaustion from her swollen eyes. "Momma?"

"There's a messenger here for you."

Tallora prayed the news was good as she roused herself. When she peeked through the porthole of her room, she saw a man wearing the sash of the royal family. Forcing a smile, she swam up. "Yes, sir?"

"Tallora," the messenger acknowledged with a polite nod, "I come with an invitation from King Merl—he asks for your presence in his summit with the Solviran Royals."

It took all her will to not burst into relieved tears. By Staella's Grace, their plan had succeeded.

"In two weeks time, an envoy shall be leaving from the palace to Solvira—you will accompany them."

"I will be there," she replied, unable to resist beaming.

The man swam away, and Tallora was left dumb at his words. She looked at her momma, smiling wide.

Her mother forced her own. "At least warn me before you decide to be wed," she said simply, and then she swam to her bedroom, leaving Tallora alone.

Two weeks was hardly any time at all, yet it felt longer than the previous six months.

Tallora worked in her mother's shop, though she spent her days thinking of Dauriel—her voice and her smile, charmed nights spent laughing and making love. Apprehension churned in her gut, the warning in her mother's words. Her disapproval had been hurtful, unexpected, but Tallora knew—she *knew*—in her heart that her momma would understand in time. She had to, though they proceeded to not speak of it at all.

Tallora missed Dauriel so, perhaps even more than her home.

Kal's visits were frequent. He brought only good tidings—news that his father had spoken to Dauriel a few times, already set aside a few fears, and perhaps even looked forward to the summit.

The Speaker would be present. Moratham had agreed.

"Dauriel did say it would be best that I not attend the summit," Tallora said on one visit to the reef, hesitant as she brushed her finger along an anemone, well used to the gentle enveloping of the digit by its pink tendrils. "For my safety, and in case anyone tried to threaten me."

Kal watched her actions, his hands kept to himself—he had made no affectionate gestures since the reveal of Tallora's true feelings, save for hugs upon their greetings and partings. "I see her point, but bear in mind that no one knows the true measure of your worth to her. I don't plan to speak of it to anyone until you do. But if you're worried, I'll tell my father to keep guards at your side. He's insistent that you be there in case you need to plead on our behalf to Solvira—he's taken to heart that you're our best asset for negotiating with Empress Dauriel."

As the anemone released her, Tallora placed her hands in her lap, watching the little creature await prey. "Do you swear he means me no harm?"

"He doesn't like you," Kal replied, an apology in his half-hearted smile, "but he's begrudgingly accepted that you're useful."

Time passed. Anxiety brewed, but Tallora resolved to simply do her best. The fate of the peace of the world relied on the words of her peers—and if it went wrong, perhaps her words too.

The night before, Tallora politely excused herself after dinner. There was somewhere her heart yearned to be.

The coral reef was too gorgeous for words, a rainbow of beauty for her to behold. The wildflowers above were lovely, but Tallora thought the anemones and coral and thousands of creatures were better by far, unafraid of her touch as she mingled among them and dared to befriend a particularly brave flounder.

This was what she would leave behind. It brought a lump to her throat.

When the morning came, Tallora hugged her mother tight, remaining for a few silent moments. "Know that I am proud of you," she whispered, and Tallora withheld a sob at that.

The decorated volcanic rock was always a sight, the palace brilliant in the fading light. Tallora nodded quickly to the guards, who let her pass.

An icy current swept through the room at her entrance. Tallora watched every eye in the throne room cast over her, condemnation in their stares. King Merl sat upon his decorated throne, a frown at his lips as she approached and bowed. Silence settled. Tallora shifted awkwardly, willing her heartbeat to steady.

"Tallora!" Like a burst of sun behind the clouds, Kal entered and swam to greet her. With no care for propriety, he engulfed her in a hug, one she returned, overjoyed to have warm company. "All is prepared. Are you ready?"

Tallora had brought only a small bag, with a comb and a few other personal effects. She nodded, then felt Kal's hand caress the bag, hanging just below her waist, and slip something inside. His smile betrayed no mischief, though he did offer a wink.

"I still hold reservations," King Merl said, his lip stiff as Kal released her. "But I have been swayed to believe this is the greatest chance for peace between our kingdoms."

"I understand," she said simply, and his demeanor softened by degrees.

"Good."

At the word, a small envoy of guards moved out, with King Merl in tow. Kal gestured for her to follow. "The people have not been informed of this.

She slipped her hand inside her bag, feeling a rounded, decorated interloper, and realized what Kal had placed inside. She gripped the mirror tight and grinned, finding him the most endearing man in all the world. "Good to know."

"The empress was kind enough to offer to conjure a portal for us, but my father declined. The summit shall be in six days, and we are due to arrive just in time."

"Good thing I hate camping," she replied, her wink hopefully conveying her jest.

Kal's infectious grin brought relief. "This will be a little more pleasant than camping."

Tallora smiled as they came upon a few waiting carriages, strapped to unruly looking seahorses, as well as a large ensemble of guards. Fifteen in all, and each looked armed and prepared for war. Advisor Chemon swam to King Merl, the duo speaking of idle semantics.

This would be a peaceful meeting, or so Tallora hoped, but the king prepared for violence all the same.

The carriage was a large ball of sorts, but with an open top, decorated with pearls and shells. Rounded benches sat within, promising a relaxing trip. Once the king had entered, Kal gestured for Tallora to follow.

All the comfort in the world couldn't detract from the cold aura within the carriage. King Merl sat in absolute silence, and thus set the precedent: when the carriage lurched, no one spoke.

The ensuing quiet was hardly peaceful, but it lingered for hours. Tallora contemplated the future.

Her mother's disapproval of Dauriel had shattered a piece of her dream, that her life might be pure bliss in the arms of the woman she loved. Whatever her affection and loyalty to Dauriel, could she simply cast her mother aside? Her only family? Tallora stubbornly swallowed her rising emotion at the thought, watching instead as schools of silver fish swam in practiced formations beyond the window, their patterns a mystery to all except them.

Perhaps her mother would come around in time, yet the idea of a wedding without her stung. Tallora wondered idly what her father would have thought and missed his laugh with all her heart. Though he'd housed depthless anguish, he'd hidden it behind a mask of humor. She recalled when she was six years old, and he had teased her when she'd proclaimed her true love for a boy at school—*"You won't need a veil for your wedding. We'd lose you in all that white hair—"*

Emotion rose; Tallora nearly choked holding back her tears and thought of harmless things instead.

They stopped a few hours later to stretch and relieve themselves. Tallora politely excused herself, her thoughts loud amidst the silent company. She longed to joke with Kal, but King Merl's stark disapproval set her on edge.

She swam a ways off, into a collection of kelp. When she glanced back, she deemed herself alone and withdrew the gifted mirror from her pocket. She tapped it, stomach fluttering when it glowed.

And there, within seconds, was Dauriel's face. The whole ocean paled to the beauty of her smile. "Hello, Tallora."

Heat blossomed across her cheeks. "Hi," she replied, for she could summon no word but that, silly as it was. "How are you?"

"Barely slept since you left," Dauriel replied, and Tallora couldn't tell if her wink meant she was jesting. The dark rings around her eyes suggested not. "Too much to prepare. If I prove nothing else at this summit, it's that I can put on a spectacle."

"I'll be happy to comment on that myself once I see it." Tallora smiled but didn't miss how Dauriel's faltered.

"You are coming, then?"

Tallora nodded. "King Merl has insisted. Kal swears he means no harm, though. He wants me there in case I need to soften you to his cause."

The background shifted behind Dauriel—perhaps she'd sat upon a chair. "Your safety will be taken into account, then. It's the most important thing to me."

There was more to say, though it threatened to break her heart. Her smile faltered. "I spoke to my mother. About us."

Something in her countenance must have revealed her truth. Dauriel's features softened. "I see."

"She has reservations," Tallora said simply, but the last word stung nonetheless. "I forget that my people have feared Solvira's shadow for centuries. I forget that I once did too. I think if my mother met you she'd understand, but . . ." Tallora shut her eyes, recalling the damning words, that she'd be betraying her own kind. "Well, needless to say the conversation didn't go the way I'd hoped."

"What will you do, then?"

Dauriel's face revealed nothing of her inner feelings. Tallora spoke the truth. "I've always followed my instincts. My heart says you're my destiny. It always has, even when I fought against it." She smiled, finding it easier than she would have thought. "Dauriel, I want to be yours. I accept—"

"Not yet." Dauriel's smile was endlessly soft, though Tallora swore she heard muted voices from beyond. "I'd prefer to hear the words when I can kiss them from your lips."

"Damn, you know how to make a girl weak," she replied, relishing Dauriel's enamor.

Longing shone in her silver gaze. "I would love nothing more than to have you stay."

Oh, the words were beautiful upon her lips. Tallora adored her so.

"Now is not a good time to speak," Dauriel said, her disappointment clear in her glower. "But will you again? I want to know you're safe on your journey."

"We'll talk every day, if you let me," Tallora replied. "Though not when I'm actually travelling— I'm in rather cold company . . ."

Then, she saw a flickering from beside her and realized she was being watched.

Chemon looked as startled as she to be seen. To the mirror, she said, "I have to go. Hopefully we will speak again soon."

Dauriel said nothing, but she did blow a kiss before tapping the mirror's reflection. The image faded, leaving only Tallora. "Enjoying eavesdropping?" she said to the interloper, letting her annoyance show.

"No, my lady, and I apologize." His polite reply did little to soothe her nerves, yet left nothing for her to say. "Simply poor timing on my part."

She merely glared as she swam away, content to return to the carriage.

Chapter XII 🐚

The days passed quickly, though in relative silence. Tallora stole moments away to hear her empress' voice, and they spoke of silly, heartfelt things—of the day to day, of wedding plans, and Tallora informed her of the exceptionally childish list of demands she'd had for a wedding as a little girl—*"I wanted Yaleris the dragon to be a witness. Momma didn't try and dissuade me, and I appreciate that."*

"I'll do my best," was Dauriel's reply, and Tallora thought her wonderful.

Amidst her joy, anxiety brewed in her gut—Chemon had heard something, but he behaved no differently. Perhaps he'd only heard the end?

When she breached the subject with Kal, his thoughtful reply soothed her troubled heart—*"Even if he knows, there's nothing he can do to stop the summit. All will be well."*

Travel was not relaxing, but on the morning of the sixth day, they arrived. Excitement welled in Tallora's stomach—before the carriage could stop, she swam to the surface, she saw the nearby shore, and when she broke above the water, a familiar face waited upon the bank.

Prince Ilaeri stood with a large ensemble of guards, looking unsurprised to see her. "Tallora," he said politely, and when more faces appeared, he greeted them.

She hardly heard it though, for what awaited upon the shore.

Tallora had risen above the lake before, knew the land around it to be smooth and untamed, but now there stood a gigantic amphitheater. A great tower had been built into the side of the lake, and Tallora realized water filled the hollow interior, contained through magic—similar to how she had been caged all those months ago. It led to a great podium facing the amphitheater, and she wondered what theatrics Dauriel had in store.

When King Merl surfaced, Ilaeri bowed. "King Merl of the Tortalgan Sea, I am Prince Ilaeri of the Solviran Crown, Advisor to Empress Dauriel. I am humbled beyond measure to greet you on this momentous day."

King Merl said, "The honor is ours as well, to be a part of the occasion."

"Accommodations have been provided to care for you and yours until sundown, when the meeting shall be held—the Speaker is due to arrive within the next few hours. Food shall be delivered upon my word, and if there is anything at all you need, I am happy to be of service."

It was a pretty speech, and Merl smiled politely. "The empress is generous. But will we be negotiating in public?"

"The empress holds high hopes for peace between us and wishes for there to be no question of it to her people." Ilaeri spared a knowing glance to Tallora before continuing his speech, but she slowly sunk into the water, even as a volley of servants appeared from the walls delivering the promised food.

Disappointment churned in her stomach. Dauriel was not here. She swam away from the rest, her hand clutching the mirror in her satchel instead as she sought a quiet place.

Amidst a craggy rock collection, she found a comfortable seat. Tallora glanced back, deemed herself alone, and withdrew the gifted mirror from her satchel. She tapped it, stomach fluttering when it glowed . . . and glowed . . .

But no one came. Frowning, she tapped again, disappointed to be met with nothing. She slipped it back into her pack, resolving to try later. Surely Dauriel had been informed of her arrival—perhaps she was simply detained. There was much to prepare for.

As the day progressed, Tallora heard swathes of people beyond.

She spent her time with Kal, mostly, touching base on a few important things. "I still do feel awful for leading you on," Tallora said as they sat upon the shore. They watched people from the city fill the amphitheater, disappearing behind its walls.

Kal and his bright eyes smiled to blind the sun. "I was disappointed. I think you're wonderful. But I'm happy to remain friends if you are."

Tallora nodded, her smile shy and relieved. "You'll have another girl within a week."

"I already had Leah," he teased, and then he stared wistfully at the city. "I wonder how she is."

Tallora winked. "Perhaps we can convince Harbinger to give her fins."

They laughed the afternoon away, as content as old times.

Near sunset, Prince Ilaeri approached the shore. "Citizens of the Tortalgan Sea, the time is near at hand. If King Merl and Prince Kalvin wouldn't mind following me, I'll show them the path up to the stage."

Tallora followed as well, leaving a small ensemble of guards and Advisor Chemon behind. A large envoy of Solviran Guards remained by the lake, perhaps to keep the peace and protect their guests.

They were led toward the great structure, and Tallora saw that if she dove, she could follow the water up the center. "There are places set for you, up there," Ilaeri said. "Empress Dauriel was adamant about making certain you sat as an equal to she and the Speaker."

Dauriel did nothing by accident, as meticulous and politically savvy a woman as Tallora had ever met. Before she could dive, Ilaeri said, "Tallora, with due respect, it's been requested that you do not join them on the stage just yet."

"And with all respect in return," King Merl said, startling Tallora when his hand settled on the small of her back, "I would prefer she stay with us." There was a threat in the words, but not to Ilaeri, no—to Tallora herself.

"I shall inform Empress Dauriel of the change," Ilaeri replied, as patient as ever with his serene voice. "Go on your way."

Though unnerved at the exchange, Tallora followed Merl and Kal, contemplating Dauriel's fears that a knife might be held to her throat. Behind her, Merl's guards watched. The unspoken threat remained. She returned the gesture, glaring as she swam up the structured tunnel, noting that the magic truly was one and the same, between this and the pen she'd once been kept in—but at a much larger scale.

When she emerged from the water, a hundred feet up, she faced a legion.

Tallora appeared on a narrow stage within an elevated pool, gazing upon a massive gathering of people. She didn't know the population of Neolan, but she swore the whole city had come to watch their empress proclaim peace before the world. Those farthest away appeared as little more than insects in the distance.

She held up a hand to protect her eyes, the setting sun illuminating the stage. A large ensemble of Solviran Guards waited at the back, all armed with spears and swords. General Khastra stood among them, her massive hammer behind her. Beside a grand throne in the center stood High Priest Rel of Ilune, his garb subdued and black—the God of Death had few sigils of finery.

At the head of the pool sat an elevated chair, one King Merl easily placed himself upon. Kal and

Tallora stayed in the water, both enthralled by the sights—Kal practically radiated excitement.

She recognized Amulon among a small gathering of Morathan soldiers surrounding a man upon a throne. Though handsome and dressed as a decadent royal should be, Tallora saw nothing particularly impressive about him. Was this the feared Speaker? The mouthpiece of Morathma? Amulon held more power in his stance.

Ascending a spiraling wooden staircase in the back corner was Empress Dauriel, unquestionably magnificent in her ensemble of black and silver, her cape billowing in the breeze. The crown upon her head bore a single onyx stone, and a subtle embroidery of silver moons lined the edges of her tunic. Her twin swords attached at her hip, unsheathed, and when she approached the edge of the stage, the crowd erupted in cheers.

Dauriel raised her arms, as though prepared to embrace them and their accolades. "Citizens of Solvira!" she cried, her voice amplified to boom across the amphitheater—unquestionably through magic. The already invigorated crowd screamed. "I welcome you to this glorious event. History shall be made this day!"

Amidst the ensuing cheers, Dauriel turned around and faced the Speaker. "Speaker of Morathma," she said darkly, and here her voice held its normal volume, "now is the time."

The words sent chills through Tallora's blood, and she watched, transfixed, as the Speaker glowed from within. Every piece of him seemed to shift—his stance, his gaze, even the pores of his skin became enveloped in a sheen of light. He stood and grew, both in height and muscled bulk. Wings of pure light burst from his back.

Tallora knew little of gods—only enough to know that they could not manifest upon this world without a host except in rare and scattered places—

like the Temple of Unity. Should the host die, the god would return to their world of Celestière.

She suddenly understood, in stark clarity, that the title of "Speaker" was literal.

Everything about him had become something new—though he bore the same face, a melding of scars covered nearly all his skin, extending down to his throat and past the open collar of his shirt. Even his hands held the same pattern, and his wings were marred in their magnificence, scarred and limp. Tallora recalled the nightmarish, burning snake and her gut-twisting fear, but to see him physically stand before her, bearing all the might of the god he was, she felt no pity at all.

He towered over them all, even Khastra, and when he spoke, it rumbled like thunder. "Empress Dauriel Solviraes," he said, offering no bow or nod or deference. Instead, he offered a large hand, and Dauriel accepted with no fear.

Though he towered above her, Dauriel held herself as an equal. "Morathma, Jewel of the Desert." They released, and the tension in the air could have sparked a flame.

Morathma looked to King Merl, and though Tallora could not see her king's face, if he felt half the shock she did, it showed. "Tortalga has quarrels with none. I respect him and his domain. Perhaps we shall leave this day as allies instead of merely acquaintances."

"I do not speak for my god," King Merl said, his tone holding nothing but respect, "but I cannot imagine this not being the first step toward an alliance."

Morathma looked to Kal, his gaze lingering as he politely nodded. When his eyes finally settled upon Tallora, she froze. "And you are the fabled mermaid, the one who brings us here today."

Morathma was not her god, but he was still a god to tremble before. She failed to find her voice; instead, she merely nodded.

He smiled, and it was charming—despite the scars visible upon his skin, there was someone handsome underneath. "It is fitting and proper that a follower of Staella would seek to bring peace. Give my regards."

Well, Kal had sought to bring peace, but Tallora wasn't going to argue with a literal deity. She nodded, but any words she might've said shriveled at the unbridled hatred marring Dauriel's visage.

It dissipated before he faced her again, but Tallora felt something terribly wrong stirring in her gut. She glanced behind to the guards, but they hadn't moved an inch. She looked below and saw no one— perhaps she could still make an escape.

"Please, have a seat," Dauriel said, gesturing to Morathma's throne. Seated, he matched her standing height, his wings floating listlessly behind him. "Your appearance shows your commitment to this cause." She looked to King Merl. "As does yours."

Her gaze settled a moment on Tallora, lingering as her bravado faded by a mere glimmer. Tallora smiled, and Dauriel matched it—not Empress Dauriel of the Solviran Crown but Dauriel alone, the one who lavished affection and loved with all the vulnerability of her delicate heart.

The woman Tallora so dearly loved. Peace settled within her.

The spell between them ended, and Dauriel became the feared empress, her silver gaze sharp as it returned to the crowd. "A few thoughts, before we begin," she said, and again her voice boomed across the amphitheater. The crowd settled into pristine silence. "I marvel at the strength and conviction of the monarchs standing beside me. I wish to apologize, before the eyes of Solvira and the witnesses of these foreign lands, for the crimes enacted by this kingdom beneath my late mother's reign."

A surprised murmur passed through the crowd. Tallora saw stark disbelief upon the faces around her—save for those from Solvira.

"I am not Vahla. She is a stain upon the Solviraes line, stripped of her titles and name by Goddess Neoma before her gruesome demise at the God of Death's hand. Solvira will not be defined by her cruelty and ineptitude—hence, my first act was to right the great wrong bringing us here today by returning Tallora, the mermaid stolen from the seas, to her home."

Dauriel spared a glance backwards. First to Tallora, who saw conviction upon her strong features, and then to Merl, and finally Morathma himself. "Still," she continued, "my mother had one talent some here might have considered a strength—her capacity to bargain. She held a commitment to peace and a willingness to compromise to get it—including to Moratham, despite a rivalry that precedes Solvira's founding." She smiled at Morathma, taking slow steps toward him. "There are many things to say about that, for the willingness to negotiate peace despite a greater feud."

Tallora watched Dauriel's motions, though her silver eyes were set upon the seated godly host—her cape billowed slightly, revealing her hands upon the hilts of her swords on her hips.

"I wouldn't say, though," Dauriel said, and though her voice lowered, it still carried into the crowd, "that any of those things are good."

Tallora's heart stopped as time slowed. Silver flame hastened Dauriel's movements—in a single, blazing motion, she swung the swords, crying out as they struck Morathma at the neck. He did not scream; he had no mouth to do so. His head fell as a separate piece.

The light within him vanished. A discorporated cry echoed across the stage and the amphitheater as Morathma dissipated into the void, banished back to the angelic realm, his host murdered by the Empress of Solvira.

The crowd erupted into raucous cries—some cheering, others in horror. Chaos ensued as Solviran soldiers swarmed upon the Morathan Envoy, slaughtering them all within seconds—save Amulon, forced to his knees, a knife set to his throat.

Tallora screamed when a great blue hand reached into the water and grabbed Kal. "I will not hurt you unless you try to escape," Khastra muttered, the threat apparent as she dragged him onto the stage, his tail useless as he flopped above water.

Priest Rel struck the king with some invisible, magical force, knocking him prone beside his son on the blood-soaked stage. "What is the meaning of this?!" he cried, but Dauriel kept her stance.

"Bargaining. Now, take them away." She stepped toward the edge of the stage, ignoring Tallora, who was too shocked to speak. Guards hauled off Kal and Merl, leaving Tallora alone in the water. "Take heed," Dauriel whispered to Amulon, "for you'll be the messenger."

She looked back to her people, bravado in her stance. "Citizens of Solvira!" Dauriel cried, furious conviction on her tongue. "I am Empress Dauriel Solviraes, and I will not be known for groveling at our enemy's feet. We are the greatest country upon this world! Will we align ourselves with the people who spit upon our goddesses?!"

She waited for the unified cries of, *"No!"* from her people.

"Who seek to steal your borders?!"

"No!"

"Who *raped* your mother goddess?!"

"No!"

"No, we will not!" Dauriel let the statement linger, the crowd's energy palpable, bursting with rage. "We have sat aside and allowed the Desert Sands to walk freely despite his crimes for too long! Now is the time, Solvira—I will not be known for my mother's bastardized legacy. I will lead us into the greatest age our kingdom has ever known!"

The crowd screamed, and the first of Tallora's tears finally fell.

"The desert shall be flooded by the blood of its people!"

Tallora could hear no more. With a sob, she dove into the water, numb as she swam down the tower. The lake engulfed her, the scenery natural instead of man-made.

She swam to the surface of the lake, the distant roaring of the crowd inescapable. Tears clouded her vision, betrayal and confusion pulsing red hot through her blood. In the far distance, she saw her own people in disarray, Solviran guards yelling unintelligible cries. The sun set, and Tallora was shadowed by night.

She trembled and perhaps would have sunk, but a quiet voice from the shore said, "Tallora . . ."

She could form no words, merely gasped as she fought to breathe. Lip quivering, she turned and saw Dauriel, her severe gaze for Tallora alone. Beyond, the crowd kept their screams, but closer still was the staircase leading to the top of the tower. Dauriel came forward, her boots sinking into the mud at the edge of the lake.

"You came to me, earnest and naïve, to tell me of a plot against my kingdom," Dauriel said, her face cruel, yet Tallora saw anguish in those beautiful eyes. "You presented proof that your kingdom had colluded with mine's sworn enemy—whose god is and always shall be at odds with yours and mine. But more than that, you asked me to choose between you and my kingdom." The empress' lip quivered; tears streamed down Tallora's face, every word true and damning all at once. "You asked me to choose between you and every single citizen who lives and dies by my word. You asked me to disgrace their heritage, to insult them by negotiating with people who have mocked and hated us for thousands of years, and ignore the atrocities being committed across our borders. Solvira is not pristine, but we don't align with the kingdom our Mother Goddess fled from; we don't affiliate with a god who decries the free will of his citizens, who would rather see a woman like you raped and sold as a slave than be with someone like me—"

"Stop it!" Tallora cried, the words tearing out of her throat. Rage filled her, pulsing hot through her blood. "Stop playing a victim! Oh, you had no choice—this is what you wanted!" Her tears fell rapidly, clouding her vision as she stared upon Dauriel Solviraes, Empress of the Fucking World. "You wanted a war. You wanted a legacy. Congratulations, you'll be known as the empress who sent her people to die in the desert over a war you think is your birthright."

Yet she remembered the burning snake, the palpable glee in the crowd to watch it smolder into ashes. Minutes ago, they had cheered for the Speaker's death, for Morathma's banishment, invigorated by Dauriel's speech.

She would leave a legacy, yes—as the empress who would deliver Morathma's head on a platter to Neoma, should she have her way. Her people would cheer her name for eternity.

Dauriel brought her palms to her eyes to ward away tears. "Yes, it's what I always wanted. Yes, I've swung the first blow. The soldiers at the border have already received their orders to march." When her hands fell to her side, her eyes were swollen and red. "But your kingdom shall live in peace, just as you wished. Your guards and advisor will be sent home with the warning that the king and heir apparent will be safe for as long as the Tortalgan Sea remains docile. When the war is over, they will be released."

Dauriel's face twisted as she swallowed her grief, her pride. "When I spoke to Neoma, she told me that the weight of my calling means to place my duty before my heart. She said the choice is mine, but the consequences are not. Perhaps if you had spoken to me alone, I could have pretended to have never heard it, but you said it before my council. You said it before my father, who is conniving and wicked, and before

Adrael, who has served three generations of Solviran monarchs and would never stand for weakness, and Khastra, who would have berated me for letting my heart dictate my actions. My title is a birthright, but the moment I falter, there will be a dagger in my back and another Solviraes to take my place."

Tallora's lip trembled as she listened, the crushing weight of guilt and anger mingling as one. "Why didn't you just tell me? You could have whispered a warning—"

"Why didn't I warn you of my impending betrayal?" Dauriel smiled, yet it held only agony. "I couldn't place you in the middle of this. You were willing to leave your people behind to be my bride, but betray them? No. That's not you. But it's what I would have been asking you to do. And what kind of choice is that?"

Yet it was the choice Dauriel had made. Conflict stirred in Tallora's head and heart. She tore her gaze away, to the splendid city before her. Her future still awaited; the choice remained.

"I love you."

Her gaze wrenched back, though Dauriel stood behind a hazy mist.

"Tallora, I *love* you. But one life can't be held above my entire populace. I would fall on my sword for you; I would never lift it again, at your will—but this is about something bigger than me. Duty over heart. Yes, I wanted this, but not more than I wanted you." Dauriel stopped her words, visibly fighting tears now, the first of them leaking a shined streak across her face. "If I thought falling on my knees and begging for your forgiveness would endear myself to you, I'd do it. But I know you. You'll do what you will either way, you beautiful, willful woman."

Yet Dauriel did fall to her knees, taking no mind to the mud caking her pristine trousers or her cape. She appeared as a supplicant in prayer, though no words left her lips. She merely stared; her silver eyes rimmed with red as her tears continued falling.

Trembling, Tallora's hand reached into her bag and withdrew the silver mirror, her link to Solvira and to Dauriel, her love. She gazed at her reflection and saw a tear-streaked mess, saw shimmering skin stained by sorrow, saw a girl who loved a warmonger whose destiny it was to take the world for her own.

It wasn't a path Tallora could follow.

Tallora slowly swam to the shore, unable to face Dauriel's gaze, and gently placed the mirror upon the muddy shore, finality in the gesture. Behind her tearful vision, she met Dauriel's eye and saw her as she truly was—empress of the world, bearing shackles of gold, ruthless and arrogant, fated to burn brilliant and bright.

It was as Dauriel had said—they did not speak of rulers who died peacefully in their beds. She would not go softly into the Beyond.

Sparing a moment to look up at the first vestiges of the starry night, she offered a silent prayer for strength: *Mother Staella, steel my heart.*

She looked to Dauriel, whose composure hung by a thread, and shook her head. She could summon nothing more.

Tallora dove into the water.

Chapter XIII 🐚

Tallora joined a somber crowd and asked in utter monotone, "Will I be arrested?"

Advisor Chemon surveyed her with visible scrutiny, and Tallora simply looked away. "That is for Queen Fauln to say."

She, the guards, and Advisor Chemon began the long journey home. Days passed in silence. She was avoided like a plague victim, and she suspected they only humored her presence because it was right—not because they wanted anything to do with her.

They stopped at a small village called Yal for shelter and rest. Tallora laid in a provided bed feeling as useless as the slugs on the seafloor.

No. Far worse. It was her word that had pushed King Merl to finally act. She had done this. She had spoken on Solvira's behalf, too enamored by love to see the wicked truth—that Solvira was a country of brutality, their empress the most brutal of all. By Staella's Grace—she had been *used*.

Yet she couldn't shake the memory of Dauriel on her knees, tears in her eyes, her silent plea for Tallora to stay anyway.

Oh, she was a fool. Behind the sting of betrayal, she wanted Dauriel. Dauriel, who was born into a role Tallora could not condone, who had used Tallora's word as a weapon for her cause. She rolled onto her side in the black night, alone in her room at the inn, yet still she wished so dearly that she was in a different room within a high tower, drenched in moonlight and kissed by a woman who adored her. Alone, they were perfect, perfect together.

Perhaps the world hadn't been meant for them. Tallora didn't sleep; she wept all through the night.

When day came, the time passed quickly, for she cried all the while. She dreaded to deliver the ill news, to tell a woman that she might never see her husband and son ever again.

Surely they neared Stelune. Tallora wondered at the scenery, the craggy rock formations bespeaking familiarity, yet she couldn't place it. There was no plantlife to speak of, no fish to admire.

In the looming silence, she gasped when someone actually spoke. "Tallora, an inquiry."

She looked up and saw fiery red locks of hair. "Yes, sir?"

Chemon swam to her side, matching her slow pace. "I've been contemplating something I overheard between you and Empress Dauriel. Did I hear correctly that she said you could be her bride?"

She might've lied, had she the will. "Yes," she whispered instead.

"The empress has a reputation for sleeping around, but it seems she's truly enamored with you."

Tallora's gut stirred in warning—something was off about his calm demeanor. Their kingdom was in crisis, yet he spoke frivolously of the hated empress? "I suppose so," she said simply. She gazed out upon the scenery. "How much farther until Stelune?"

"Not too much."

"We are going to Stelune, right?"

Chemon raised a single, amused eyebrow. "Where else would we be going?"

Tallora studied the rugged terrain, the rock formations bearing lengthy cracks. She looked at the night sky and wished she could justify swimming up to gaze upon the stars and navigate their way home.

The rocks were as black as onyx, and within one particularly lengthy crack, she swore she felt radiating heat. She did recognize the shattered terrain, though it had been entirely ravaged. This wasn't home. This was the Great Fire Trenches, destroyed in Harbinger's earthquake.

Panicked, Tallora swam as fast as her tail could take her—

Until strong arms gripped her fins. She cried out, pain striking her as a man wrenched her back. "Let me go—!"

Something hard smacked her head. Her struggling ceased, despite her efforts—she could hardly see straight, dizziness overtaking her senses.

"This doesn't have to be difficult," Chemon said, his hair unmistakable despite her hazy sight. Arms wrapped around her torso; though she flailed about, she could not escape. Blood seeped into the water. "I have no intention of killing you, unless you force our hand."

Again, pain struck her head. Limp, her blood pounded in her ears, vision swimming as the guard dragged her body through the water. She grasped consciousness like a rock in a typhoon yet feared it might be futile. Braided kelp tied her wrists together.

She blinked in and out of consciousness, feeling the sky darken, the water grow colder...

And then, in pure darkness, she awoke.

Tallora sat up, careful to avoid bashing her head upon any unseen rocks. "Hello?" she called, and from afar, she heard scuffling.

A light suddenly illuminated the scene, casting the cave in shades of red and orange. Chemon approached, holding a glowing crystal, revealing the craggy walls, as well as the bonds restraining her arms and tail. "Glad to see you awake."

"What the fuck are you doing?" she said, the red of his hair nearly glowing in the ambient light.

"Come here," Chemon said, beckoning to a distant figure. Tallora recognized him as a guard. More followed—she was surrounded by men. "Tallora, you've made yourself a person of exceptional interest, and I should have guessed that you would be the key to saving the seas."

"I beg your pardon?" There was little Tallora could do to move, so when two men approached, she could only cower, braided kelp ropes digging deep into her skin and scales.

189

"Empress Dauriel is not someone to be trusted," Chemon continued, something leering in his gaze, "but I do trust *you*, Tallora. I trust that your heart is truly broken and that you've fallen into a love affair with the most powerful woman in the world. And when I told King Merl what I overheard when you spoke to the mirror, he said to hold to that in case of the worst. He said to act."

Tallora merely stared, not understanding at all.

"Take her," he said. Tallora struggled against the guards' grip, but with her tail bent and tied, her arms behind her back, there was little she could do to resist except curse and try to bite. "You're going to save the seas, girl. Willingly or not."

She was carried through a dark tunnel, lit only by the crystal in Chemon's hand. Not once did she cease her struggle, but even when she managed to free herself of their grip, she was scooped up again.

The cave opened up into a massive, familiar amphitheater. Before a great pit of lava stood a mural, carved in stone, depicting an image of a single eye and a thousand tentacles. Runes—Demoni and Celestial both—were etched around the depiction, and Tallora felt the eye follow her wherever she went.

Behind them, the rest of the guards spread out, some marveling at the mural just as she did. "I consulted an Onian Witch named Yoon," Chemon said, stopping before the great eye, gazing upon it in wonder, "who claimed she knew nothing of the key to her father's prison. Do you know what lies behind this wall, Tallora?"

"A monster," she spat, still twisting in her bonds. "A monster named Yu'Khrall who once nearly destroyed the Tortalgan Sea."

"All true, yet you've spectacularly missed the point. Solvira cannot be reasoned with, and perhaps you see that now. Merl faltered in that belief for one moment, and look at him. Your ideas are infectious, and I contemplated having you assassinated for your foolish tongue. Yu'Khrall is the protection we need.

We simply need leverage—and with Moratham's aid, we're prepared to offer him a mighty boon."

"You can't reason with him! I spoke to Yoon, who said—"

"Yoon is a fool of a witch," Chemon said with a dismissive wave. "All presentation with no substance. Not even she knew the answer we sought. If she is the future of Onias' progeny, perhaps he shall cease to be great. But Yu'Khrall—"

"Was placed in here *by Neoma!*" Tallora twisted; she managed to dislodge herself, only for a new set of guards to apprehend her. "The gods had to intervene the last time!"

"Where are the gods, then? They haven't come to aid us against Solvira. Tortalga is a hermit who turns away from his people, and Staella is busy tempering the woman who oppresses us. Sometimes, the gods can't save us, Tallora. We must save ourselves." He swam toward her; she held his hateful gaze and said nothing

"Only the Heart of Silver Flame may break the seals," he continued. "Rather cryptic. We were baffled for months, and up on the land, scholars in Moratham studied every text they could to try and solve the puzzle. They even sent the literal heart of one of their Priestesses of Staella—when she died a natural death, we were assured—to see if it might be the key. We truly did lose hope and thought only Goddess Staella herself could open the seal until . . . the strangest thing happened."

Intrigue crossed the advisor's face as he stared upon the mural. "The answer came as a vision the night you and Prince Kalvin returned from Solvira. I remember waking as cold as ice, the feeling of dread inescapable yet . . . that voice—"

"You're doing this because of a fucking dream?" She tried in vain to wrench herself away, still overpowered by the guards.

"Not a dream—a *vision*. A vision detailing the poetic nature of Neoma's thinking, that for all her tyrannical ambition, there is one whose wisdom she holds in the highest regard, the only angel capable of reasoning with her. And so of course she would not keep that power for herself or her descendants—it is not in her nature, or so the vision said. The power to free Yu'Khrall is delegated to only one person, whether they know it or not. The vision said to said to seek Neoma's heart upon this realm; we need their blood." Chemon's smile held victory, and this time he joined in helping to lift Tallora by the arms. "And how convenient, Tallora, follower of Staella, that you should be revealed as the beloved of her chosen descendent. Empress Dauriel intended to marry you, yes? If you are not the key, then there is none."

Panic filled her, the insanity of their plan liable to get her killed—and the whole sea, if they were right. "If it truly is a vision, you don't know who sent it. You don't know what you're dealing with," she said, but in their grips, she had no hope to escape. She tired; the bonds lacerated her skin; and her heart lay heavy, back in Solvira. She spoke the hateful words, but she merely fell limp.

"Perhaps it is nothing—but I have nothing to lose by shedding a drop of your blood." They carried her to the mural, toward the great eye dominating the wall. Close now, Tallora marveled at the detail, the patterns precise and deliberate, hardly marred by time. The eye stood twice her height, perfectly centered upon the massive wall.

Chemon withdrew a knife; Tallora cried out when he slashed it across her palm. Something sharp pierced the skin of her wrist as her bonds suddenly broke. "Touch the center of the eye," Chemon continued, his beguiling tone chilling her blood. She could not speak—all her willpower went to withholding her tears from the stinging in her hand. His grip returned to her arm. "Do it willingly, and you'll have righted the wrong you created. The sea will not retaliate against Solvira for as long as they hold our king and prince hostage—you truly have ruined us. But do this one thing, and I give you my sworn oath your name shall be cleared."

Tallora rapidly shook her head. No matter how shattered her heart might be, whatever her crimes, this wasn't a cause to sell her soul for. "I won't damn my home by summoning a monster."

"You trust the Onian Witch?"

"I do—" An elbow struck her forehead. Dizziness stole her focus. Tallora couldn't fight when Chemon touched her hand to the center of the ominous eye.

Where she touched, a thousand cracks appeared beneath it, stained a deep maroon. They spread from her fingers, slowly etching bloodied lines into the rock. Though Tallora wrenched her hand back, the damage had been done.

The cracked lines glowed. The cavern shook. When the mural crumbled, Chemon laughed, his delight palpable. Dread flowed through Tallora's veins—by every god, his vision had been true.

Whose hands had he played into?

A massive cave lay revealed. Chemon swam inside; the guards followed, dragging her along.

From the faint light of the crystal, Tallora saw eerie shadows deep within, illuminating what she thought might be a gigantic serpent, coiled and trapped. It flinched at the light, shifting at their approach, and Tallora realized the serpent's body was thicker than someone twice her height.

Still, the cavern shook, and Tallora's heart screamed to flee. She struggled against the guards, when a sudden *booming* crushed her down to her core. Vicious words, spoken in a language that burned her ears, rattled the walls. The hands upon her released— Tallora floated to the ground, struggling against the bonds still tying her tail to her back.

"Oh, Great Yu'Khrall!" Chemon cried, ecstasy written upon his shadowed face. "The seas bless your return!"

The ropes pinched and stung, but still Tallora fought, dread seeping through her veins.

"The very monster who shut you in here seeks to take your home next! I ask you—nay, implore you—as a member of the Tortalgan Court, for your aid!"

The coils shifted. Something glowed beyond, something sickly and yellow, and Tallora gazed into the abyss—

And by Staella's Grace—she was met with an eye.

"Save my people, and you shall have the empress to consume—"

A coiled appendage shot out, immediately engulfing Chemon in its great mass. Tallora heard a muffled scream as it withdrew into the mass of writhing flesh—

And then a faint *crunch.*

It was no serpent. Horror filled her as she ripped the final piece of her bonds away. Those were tentacles.

"I have no time for little mortals," a great voice boomed. The cavern rumbled; Tallora darted away as fast as she could—

Only to hear screams behind her. She dared to glance back and saw multiple appendages withdrawing and grasping the soldiers.

She daren't scream, lest she draw its attention. She swam, her sore tail steering her through the lava-filled cavern, just as multiple tentacles slowly reached out from behind her.

"I smell you." One came near enough to disrupt the water around her. She darted below and around, steering toward the small tunnel. *"Let me ... look at you."*

Tallora saw nothing in the dark terrain. She recalled the hours of wandering with Harbinger and Kal and pressed against an indent in the wall instead.

Something massive brushed the rock beside her, slowly moving to fill the tunnel. She shut her eyes, willing away tears, as she cowered against the stone. *"Mother Staella, deliver me,"* she breathed, inaudible save for the waves.

Again, the cavern shook, and from afar Tallora heard evidence of it crumbling. A mighty *crack* threatened to deafen her as the cave split apart; the very earth shifted behind her, creating a hole. Something smooth brushed against her nose. She darted into the hole, though she felt the appendage twitch.

She could see nothing, only felt the rocks around her. At any moment she could be crushed, but she swam upward, her hands clutching the wall lest she scrape away her skin and scales. Her stomach knew which direction was up.

Another rumble. An earthquake shook the stone as Tallora cowered against her rocky enclosure. She looked up, *and by Staella's Grace she saw light.*

She swam faster, the passage narrowing as she went. When her tail became encased in stone, she wrenched it forward, crying out as she lost scales, blood seeping into the water—

But she broke free.

Tallora appeared in open water, the rocky terrain beneath her. Still, the water pulsed from the earth's rumbling. She darted down the mountain, seeking not distance but shelter. Behind, the great crack in the mountain split wider, the first evidence of tentacled appendages slipping out. Tallora's body ached, yet she darted away faster—

Before her, the earth burst. Tallora gasped as a massive tentacle shot up before her, others quickly joining it, and pressed their ends to the earth—for leverage, she realized.

This monster sought to escape. Tallora darted around the tentacles, terror steering her as she swam faster.

The path ended in a sudden ravine. Tallora dove down, ignoring the coral reef beyond.

A deafening *boom* echoed across the ocean. Massive rocks slowly rained upon her as she sought refuge in the crevice. A small alcove became her sanctuary—deep below the sea, with only the light far above to see, Tallora hid as boulders slowly sunk down into the depths before her.

The sky darkened. Tallora dared to peek out and saw a monster from the depths of Onias' Hell pass over, its size unfathomable—larger than the palace in Neolan, than the lake beside the city, perhaps even larger than Stelune. It floated as a gargantuan cloud, hundreds of tentacles undulating high above as it swam above the canyon. Slow moving, but move it did, as an unstoppable force.

At the center of the mass of tentacles and other eldritch appendages, Tallora saw an enormous, unblinking eye, shining in shades of brilliant gold, with a gaping, beak-like maw beside it, far larger than she.

Hidden in her alcove, Tallora watched the shadow finally pass.

It moved toward Stelune.

Epilogue 🐚

Three weeks before Yu'Khrall's release...
Burning incense stung Khastra's eyes, the smoke wafting in swirling tendrils, caressing her face like a lover. Potent and sanguine, the unmistakable scent of lily wafted against her nostrils—a flower of death, to honor and remember.

Khastra knelt before an altar of bones in a dark, vacant room, cleared at her command. Unease filled her, yet she was war incarnate, born upon this earth. War had nothing to fear from Death.

War and Death had everything to gain from the other.

The lights snuffed out, save the flickering embers within the stick of incense. Khastra shut her eyes, steeling her breath at the soft caress upon the back of her neck.

"I was not expecting you," came the whisper, and when Khastra opened her eyes, light from behind cast an image of an angel of death, her glowing wings spreading from Khastra's own shadowed silhouette. In some realms, they stood on equal footing, but here in Ilune's Temple, Khastra was the supplicant, pledged to her glory. And so she kept her head bowed as the light shifted, revealing an illuminate hand, nearly humanoid, cast in pure light. Her hand had never left Khastra's neck—it trailed sensuously across her skin, until her hand lightly grasped Khastra's jaw, bidding her to look up.

In nearly nine thousand years of life, Khastra had never seen so wicked and lovely a smile. All of Ilune was beauty, the intoxicating, tempting embrace of death, honey to a fly. "I come with questions. I am told you may have the answers."

Ilune's finger left a lingering caress upon her jaw, and it took every ounce of discipline Khastra had to not steal her hand and kiss each perfect digit.

"Anything for you." When Khastra tried to rise, Ilune set her hand upon her shoulder, gently pushing back down. "No, stay. I like you like that."

Khastra could have fought it—Ilune was a deity, but Khastra's blood bore its own demonic powers, her godly mother made manifest—yet Ilune's true strength lay in her gaze. Khastra might as well have been in chains, yet she nearly smiled. "The mermaid girl returned."

"Oh?"

Khastra told her all—of Tallora's return, of the merfolks' foolish proposition, but finished with Yoon's appearance and the intrigue she brought. "Yoon could say no more, because of the curse upon her. But she alluded there was more to know and that you could be of help."

Ilune paced, her silken robe swishing around her legs, revealing the long line of her thigh. "So the Tortalgan Sea seeks to free Yu'Khrall. How?"

"The legend says your birth mother is the only one with the power to free Yu'Khrall. If they have no way to act, there is no danger. Yet, Yoon has alluded there is danger."

The incense snuffed out, the last of its sweet smoke and light dissipating—only Ilune herself illuminated the spacious room. She slowly shook her head, intrigue radiating from the glint in her large eyes. "There truly isn't, from the sound of it—unless someone were to tell them the missing piece."

"You are being coy."

Ilune's chuckle filled the room, her translucent wings casting ever-shifting light throughout. "Oh, assuredly."

"Tell me what I must do to prevent this monster's return."

Again, Ilune laughed, musical and light. "Khastra, darling, if only Yoon had your conviction— from the sound of it, the witch had plenty of opportunities to stop this whole affair, but she did not act. And you shall not either."

Khastra frowned, though not from anger. Ilune was not someone she could be angry with. "What shall I do then?"

"Nothing." Ilune's good humor faded, leaving only a grin as damning as sin. "I know you despise subterfuge. I would never ask anything damning of you."

"This is about stopping a monster from returning to the seas. I would—"

"Do you trust me, darling?"

Khastra dared to look up and fearlessly met the gaze of a woman for whom she would march to the gates of hell. Oh, she was wondrous—her power and beauty unparalleled—and Khastra was helpless, subdued beneath her gaze. "No," she whispered, and it was the truth, but it bore no slight on her devotion.

Ilune offered a hand. Khastra accepted, standing tall—perfectly matched to her godly counterpart, whom she faced eye to eye. "Patience," Ilune cooed, mere inches from her face. "All shall be made clear soon."

Khastra's blood pounded. She nodded, helpless to Ilune's will.

The God of Death smiled. "Trust that this is all according to plan."

The End

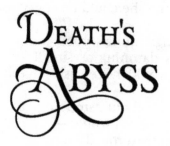

Death's Abyss

All are equal in death.

Tallora's world ends in a single, bloodstained night, and all the world will fall in line unless the gods interfere. But divine aid comes at a price no mortal can pay, except in death . . . and perhaps Death herself has a few tricks of her own.

From the author of FALLEN GODS comes a tale of redemption and sacrifice—and the true power of forgiveness.

The final installment of SEA AND STARS, *Death's Abyss*, will be available in July of 2020!

Thank you so much for reading!

SEA AND STARS began as a silly 'what if?' short story but quickly evolved into something more.

If you liked what you read, leave a review! That's the best thanks an author can get.

Can't wait for more? I have two FREE short stories available exclusively through my newsletter—one involving a certain General of the Solviran Army (being technically demoted and going on a date with an absolutely oblivious angel) and another about the protagonist of the FALLEN GODS series discovering she's a witch and spending her days with her wolf mentor. Go to sdsimper.com for more info!

Also, check me out on social media! You'll get all the latest updates. Plus you can meet other fans of SEA AND STARS, FALLEN GODS, and more! I'm @sdsimper on Facebook, Twitter, and Instagram.

See you next time, for *Death's Abyss!*

-S D Simper

About the author:

S D Simper has lived in both the hottest place on earth and the coldest, spans the employment spectrum from theatre teacher to professional editor, and plays more instruments than can be counted on one hand. She and her beloved wife share a home with their three cats and innumerable bookshelves.

Visit her website at sdsimper.com to see her other works, including *The Sting of Victory,* the dark, romantic tale of a girl who falls in love with a monster.

9 781952 349157